All the evils of the world were in this box.

Pandy shook it.

It really didn't look all that terrifying.

And then, the idea flew into her head.

What if she took the box to school for the big project?

Of course, she wouldn't open it.

Duh.

No, there was no way...what if she dropped it? Or accidentally left it in her school cupboard? Or left it in the sun and the great seal started to melt?

She looked at the box again. It was a *neato* example of the gods' enduring presence and nobody—nobody—would have anything else like it.

She would be so careful . . .

PANDORA
Gets Jealous

MYTHIC MISADVENTURES
BY CAROLYN HENNESY

Pandora Gets Jealous
Pandora Gets Vain
Pandora Gets Lazy

PANDORA
Gets Jealous

BOOK I

CAROLYN HENNESY

BLOOMSBURY
CHILDREN'S
BOOKS

NEW YORK · BERLIN · LONDON

Copyright © 2008 by Carolyn Hennesy
First published by Bloomsbury U.S.A. Children's Books in 2008
Paperback edition published in 2009

Published by Bloomsbury U.S.A. Children's Books
175 Fifth Avenue, New York, New York 10010

The Library of Congress has cataloged the hardcover edition as follows:
Hennesy, Carolyn.
Pandora gets jealous / by Carolyn Hennesy.—1st U.S. ed.
p.   cm.
Summary: Thirteen-year-old Pandy is hauled before Zeus and given six months to
gather all of the evils that were released when the box she brought to school as her
annual project was accidentally opened.
ISBN-13: 978-1-59990-196-1 • ISBN-10: 1-59990-196-X (hardcover)
1. Pandora (Greek mythology)—Juvenile fiction. 2. Mythology, Greek—
Juvenile fiction. [1. Pandora (Greek mythology)—Fiction. 2. Mythology,
Greek—Fiction. 3. Gods—Fiction. 4. Goddesses—Fiction. 5. Adventure
and adventurers—Fiction.] I. Title.
PZ7.H3917Pan 2008   [Fic]—dc22   2007023975

ISBN-13: 978-1-59990-291-3 • ISBN-10: 1-59990-291-5 (paperback)

Book design by Donna Mark
Typeset by Westchester Book Composition
Printed in the U.S.A. by Quebecor World Fairfield
3 5 7 9 10 8 6 4 2

For Donald

Σ'αγαπώ

PROLOGUE

There was a time, during the golden age of men and gods, when mankind became forgetful, almost to the point of its own destruction. Insolent and disrespectful, the twelve great Olympians thought. People had begun to take the gods' benevolence for granted and became utterly lazy. They were either forgetting to make the proper sacrifices to the gods or using the worst parts of the lambs and goats—the entrails, bones, and skin— while saving the best parts for their own feasts. Zeus, the king of the gods, eventually became so enraged at mankind's brazen insolence that he removed fire from the earth, thereby throwing mankind into nothing but endless freezing darkness.

Prometheus, the Titan, saw mankind's distress and ascended Mount Olympus to steal fire back. When Zeus saw tiny specks of orange flame lighting the black earth below, he hunted Prometheus, captured him, and chained the Titan to a rock on the side of the mountain. Each day, an enormous eagle would gorge upon Prometheus's liver. Each night, because he was immortal, his liver would grow back again. And so his torment went for years and years . . . and years . . . and years.

Eventually, Zeus's heart softened at the pleading of his son Hercules, and he agreed that Prometheus had finally paid his debt to the gods . . . with one small caveat. One tiny condition.

After Zeus allowed Hercules to break Prometheus's chains, Prometheus was summoned to the great hall of Olympus. Zeus gave him a piece of Prometheus's own liver as a reminder of his punishment for the theft of fire. And Zeus also gave him a small wooden box.

In it, each of the great gods had placed an evil or plague that, if set free, would bring torment and sorrow on mankind.

Forever.

Prometheus had watched as Jealousy, Vanity, and five other horrible plagues were dropped in one by one, including the greatest plague of all: Fear. Zeus was about to close the lid and imprint his great seal when a cry went up from the assembled gods.

"Father," said Athena, Goddess of Wisdom, stepping forth. "Should this seal ever be broken, mankind will be lost to a world of sorrow. We beseech you to also put into the box a source of comfort for mankind. Something that will allow every human the desire to go on living, even though the burden will be heavy."

"What do you suggest, daughter?" asked Zeus.

From her sky-colored cloak Athena withdrew something she held close in her hand. As she released her fingers, a fine silver mist floated slowly and gently upward. She blew softly and the mist drifted across the room and slipped into the wooden box.

"Hope," she said. "I include Hope as a gift to mankind. This and this alone will be their sole comfort in times of misfortune."

With that, Zeus closed the box and brought his mighty hand down upon the hot red wax, sealing it.

He turned to Prometheus.

"Be ever grateful that I have released you from your chains. That you should never forget your punishment, I entrust this box to you. You will guard these plagues for the rest of your days, and should my seal be broken, your torment and the torment of those you hold dear is something to be feared."

Prometheus was tormented and troubled.
And then he married.
And then he had a daughter.

And then . . .

she turned thirteen.

CHAPTER ONE
Newly "Maid"

"You have not been excused!"

Thirty-seven jaws dropped wide open.

"By all the gods on Olympus, the first one who stands will very, very much wish she hadn't!"

Normally, Master Epeus had a quality to his voice that caused every maiden in his class to doze peacefully in the olive grove for the six hours of lessons each day, but now his voice zinged and caromed off the trees like stones from a slingshot gone astray. Each girl froze; those who were almost standing bent their knees and hunched their shoulders. No one more so than the girl farthest back of the group . . . the one with plain brown hair and a slight overbite.

Master Epeus cleared his throat, sunk his head into his shoulders, and dragged his lips across his yellow teeth. Many of the girls instantly thought of an old, slow-moving but vicious bird.

"I know what the school sundial says and I know tomorrow is a big day for all, so I shall be brief . . ."

Silent groans went up all around. Brief was the one thing their teacher was not.

"I have been instructing young maidens at this academy for over sixty years and I have seen many interesting and unique things brought in for the annual project, but never once in that time has *my* class taken home any honors for originality, intellect, or effort. No first-place laurel wreath, no honorable mention sheepskin scroll, not even a 'nice try' stone tablet. Do you see my name carved in the wall of honor that leads to the amphitheater? No, I don't think so. By the smile of the great Aphrodite, if this class does not garner at least one prize tomorrow, at least one bronze medallion, there will be daily quizzes on *Euclid's Elements* of geometry with emphasis on the polyhedra, a five-hundred-page essay entitled 'Why I Love Sophocles' due next week, and all classes will be taught indoors from now on."

Three girls gasped out loud.

"And one of you lucky little things will be chosen each week to clean my toenails at the end of every day, and we all know who will have that honor first."

Everyone turned to look at the brown-haired maiden. She cast her eyes downward, poking at a lizard tail with her sandal.

"Better watch it, Pandy!" hissed one girl nearby.

"Do not congregate here in the olive grove tomorrow," Master Epeus continued. "I expect to see each and every one of you in the amphitheater and on time! Any tardiness will be dealt with severely."

Master Epeus then trained his sharp, hawkish eyes on Pandora.

"Perhaps I should have mentioned earlier that I was expecting greatness from you, but I have no fears. Not one! And I look forward to seeing the new, fascinating, but most important, *new* things you will have brought in for your project. Good day to you all. Great is Greece!"

"Good day, Master Epeus. Great is Greece," echoed the class.

Pandora adjusted her toga and robe; sitting so long on the hard ground of the olive grove made the fabric stick ever so slightly to the back of her legs. Alcie and Iole walked over, Alcie picking a fallen twig out of her hair.

"Hermes' teeth," Alcie began, leading the three of them into the crowd of girls all now leaving the school, "that was pretty obvious."

"I'll say," said Iole. "He was looking right at you."

"Yeah, well," began Pandora, "he didn't have to make such a big deal about it. I have no intention of bringing—ow!"

She was suddenly bonked on top of her head by a hard red . . . something.

Blood had begun sprinkling from the sky over ancient

Athens. It wasn't actual blood, however: each drop was in fact a brilliant red ruby.

But rubies falling out of the heavens were so commonplace nowadays that Pandora Atheneus Andromaeche Helena (Pandy to almost everyone) and her best friends Alcie and Iole didn't even bother to pick one up. They each had basketfuls back home.

"What's going on up there this time?" Iole said, squinting into the sky.

Pandy tucked her straight, plain brown hair behind her ears and looked up.

"Bellerophon and Pegasus are fighting the fire-breathing Chimera," she replied.

"Again?" Alcie said. "Flames of Tartarus, that's the third time this week! Bell's really working hard for his big hero paycheck."

"My dad thinks there might be a whole family of Chimera attacking farms and crops all over Greece," Pandy answered as another big blood ruby bonked her head again. Suddenly they were in the middle of a ruby hailstorm.

"We'd better be ready to duck if it falls out of the sky," Pandy said, covering her head with her book sack.

Alcie puffed her chest out a bit. "Well, if *my* dad were up there, it would be dead by now."

Iole choked a little as she giggled.

"Puh-leeze," Pandy laughed, "your father would be

lucky just to stay on the horse! An ordinary man can't kill a Chimera, you have to be a hero!"

At that moment Pegasus, an enormous milky white horse, steam flying from his nostrils, swooped out of the clouds, folded his huge silver-tipped gray wings, laying them neatly across his flanks, and came to rest a few feet away. On his back sat Bellerophon, the only man in all of Greece able to tame him.

"Hey, Pandora," Bellerophon said. "Alcie. Iole."

"Hi, Bellerophon," Pandy replied. "How's it going up there?"

"Not bad," Bellerophon replied, readjusting his leather hair band and snagging the unruly curls out of his eyes. "It's a big one, but nothing Pegasus and I can't handle."

Suddenly, out of the corner of her eye, Pandy saw Tiresias the Younger trudging home with a few other boys from the Apollo Youth Academy. Her heart skipped a huge beat.

"Yeah . . . uh-huh . . . well, that's really . . . um . . . ," Pandy said, watching Tiresias as he disappeared over a hill. Tiresias the Younger was, in Pandy's opinion (and she didn't care if anybody else thought so . . . although everybody did) the cutest youth in Athens. He was also the only one who made her tongue stick to the roof of her mouth whenever he was around.

"It's got an extra set of teeth, this one," Bellerophon

said, aware that Pandy was no longer paying any attention, "and spiked scales. On every scale, a spike! And an extra claw on each talon! Your father would be impressed."

"Bellerophon." Pandy focused again, now that Tiresias was gone. "When you're done . . . if you're not dead, I mean . . . could I get some of the white meat? Dad roasted a Chimera haunch last week for evening meal and *wow*! Totally dee-licious!"

"So Bellerophon, how long you gonna hide down here?" Alcie asked.

Iole nudged Alcie in the ribs.

Stunned into silence, Bellerophon slowly turned his gaze on Alcie.

"Hide?" he managed to whisper.

Pegasus shot a wad of horse-spittle in Alcie's direction.

"I'm not hiding!" Bellerophon squealed. "I was giving Pegasus a rest, for Olympus' sake. But if this is the thanks I get . . . well, I'll just kill the thing and won't bother you anymore!"

He tugged on the reins, muttering under his breath that the citizens of Athens were so hard to please. The next instant both horse and rider flew up into the clouds, quickly becoming a tiny speck.

"Okay, bye," Pandy said, watching him soar. "Dark meat is good, too!"

Ever since she had turned thirteen and had officially become a maiden, Pandora Atheneus Andromaeche Helena, only daughter of the Titan Prometheus, was bored to tears. Well . . . not bored *exactly* . . . but she couldn't quite put her finger on *what* she was feeling.

And this was another typical day. Which meant that it was horribly, devastatingly, crushingly boring, and there was absolutely *nothing* to do. She looked skyward and saw Bellerophon, now a tiny speck, rocketing about on his magnificent winged horse. Gods, how exciting that must be! And there were other heroes, men and women, all over Greece doing wonderful, brave, death-defying things right at that very moment. Hercules. Perseus. Jason and his Argonauts stealing the Golden Fleece! Her curiosity rose inside her like steam. What would it feel like to have a sword in her hand or to fly on the back of a magical animal? And Bellerophon had been right in front of her; she could have asked him for a ride sometime. How she wished she'd spoken up, just so she could have some kind—any kind—of adventure. Stupid. Stupid!

She kicked aimlessly at a blood ruby as she, Alcie, and Iole walked home from the Athena Maiden Middle School. She felt a large pimple forming on the side of her nose and slumped even further inside her school toga, dragging her book sack on the ground, almost spilling her writing stylus and sheets of papyrus.

Alcie had been grumbling that she was never going to understand Euclidian geometry and how she wished their teacher, Master Epeus, would take a long dive into the nearest lake. As she started complaining again, Alcie realized that Pandy wasn't paying attention.

"Pandy, what's wrong now?" she asked. She stopped in the middle of the chariot road, her brownish green eyes narrowing in frustration.

"I have an appointment with my tooth physician," Pandy said, brushing her hair out of her eyes, staring at the midwinter sky.

"Great!" Alcie said. "Maybe he'll tell you that your overbite is no big deal and all they have to do is yank a few teeth or put you in a horse bridle for a few months."

"Oh, wonderful," said Pandy. "Like I don't already totally look like our lead chariot stallion!"

"Our physician did that to my big brother and our family goat," said Iole, dragging a little behind as usual. "They both look fine, but my brother only likes to eat out of a feed bag now."

Pandy turned around. "I don't look like a horse!"

"I never said you did," said Iole quietly.

"She never said you did, Pandy," said Alcie.

Pandora stopped and sat beside a crumbling stone wall and looked at her friends.

Alcie and Pandy had grown up together, almost like sisters, while Iole was the newcomer. Iole's father had brought his family over from Crete when Iole was seven, and at first Pandy and Alcie were reluctant to accept her. Iole was small and frail and even now sometimes she couldn't keep up as the three girls strode through the marketplace or the olive orchards or swam in nearby lakes and rivers. But she was smart as a whip, often using big words when she spoke; not to show off, but only because her brain couldn't come up with anything smaller. It was only after she'd been moved up a year into their class that Pandy and Alcie came to love Iole (especially after she started helping them with calculus homework).

"I just don't want to go home," Pandy said. "My mom's still working a lot of overtime in her new job as Zeus's chief personal aide, so I'll probably have to babysit, and my little brother's a major pain. I *so* don't want to go to the physician. Plus, I still don't know what I'm going to bring for tomorrow's big school project."

"Yeah," said Alcie. " 'The Enduring Presence of the Gods in Our Daily Life.' Puh-leeze."

"More like, 'What Have the Gods Done for You Lately?' " said Iole. "But Pandy, I thought you had it all worked out!"

Pandy sighed. "I did, sort of. But everything I wanted to bring was dumb. And I kept getting sidetracked. It's like I have one idea and that leads to a thousand million more, and I want to know about them *all*."

"You can't fool me," Iole said, the corner of her mouth turning up just a little. "You've been cogitating about Tiresias the Younger. I saw you watching him walk home from school just now, and I've seen the stylus doodles on your papyrus folder."

"Tiresias the Yummy!" Alcie laughed.

"Cut it out . . . ," said Pandy, her cheeks coloring.

"Well," said Alcie, "you've had two moons to figure it out, so it had better be something pretty fantabulous. My dad finally agreed to let me borrow his wooden strap-on toes. He's gonna stay home tomorrow and not walk around."

"Yes, and explain to me how that's an example of the enduring presence of the gods?" said Iole.

Alcie sighed. "My dad lost his toes in the last war. Wars are started by Ares, God of—duh—War. Therefore, Ares is responsible for my dad not being able to walk right. Enduring presence. Thank you very much."

"That's more for *his* life. What about your life?" said Iole.

"Believe me, the whole family feels the enduring presence . . . like, all the time."

"I've decided to go with my original plan," said Iole.

"You? You're presenting you?" asked Alcie.

"I'm the best example I could think of. I was so sick once on Crete that everyone had pretty much given up on me. Except my mom. She kept the altar to Apollo burning all the time. She never left my side and said prayer after prayer. One night, when I was almost dead, I mean actually about to cross the river Styx, she swears she saw Apollo in my room, touching my cheek. The next day my fever was down, and I was fine two weeks later. I'm the enduring presence."

"Where's the proof?" asked Pandy.

"I'm here, aren't I? It's just classic god stuff," she said softly. "They just have to take my mom's word . . . or not."

"Well, I gotta have something great to show," Pandy muttered.

"Please don't bring your dad's liver again. Master Epeus will absolutely give you a delta. You're not, are you?" asked Iole.

"Gods no! I've brought it so many times . . . plus everybody already knows the whole stupid story: '. . . and Zeus gave Dad a big piece of his liver in a jar so that he would always be reminded, blah, blah, blah,'" said Pandy. "It's dumb."

"And it's totally and completely gross," sniggered Alcie.

"Yeah, well," Pandy said offhandedly, "at least people can look at stuff from my family and not turn to stone."

Alcie stepped back, looking like Pandy had struck her. She hung her head, her jaw clenched tight.

Iole looked nervously from one to the other.

"I can't help it if . . . ," Alcie began, then stopped. She

hoisted her schoolbag over her shoulder and walked away down the chariot road.

"Pandy," whispered Iole, "that was mean."

"Oh, Gods," Pandy said. She ran off after Alcie, wedging a stone in her sandal. "Alcie! Ow! Wait . . . Ow! Wait!"

Alcie stopped, her back still turned.

Alcestis Artemisia Medusa had turned thirteen only a few weeks before Pandy. With her red hair and brown-green eyes she was prettier than most and was having a much easier time with all the maiden stuff. Alcie's father, a wealthy man with his own business that specialized in building private backyard ruins that looked "exactly like the real thing," bought all the latest toga clasps, hair irons, and ankle bracelets for his daughter, so she always looked rather lovely . . . on the outside.

However, Alcie was also a distant niece of the great Gorgon Medusa, a creature so hideous that anyone who looked into its eyes would immediately turn to stone. Even looking at a *piece* of Medusa would turn the strongest man into a rock. A young hero, Perseus, had cut off Medusa's head some years earlier, so at least all the relatives didn't have to worry about Medusa showing up for feast days, but Alcie was still embarrassed by the blot on the family name.

Pandy clomped over to her.

"I'm sorry. I'm so sorry. I keep thinking that my family

is so much more messed up than anyone else's that it doesn't matter . . . but I'm sorry."

"Your family? Oh . . . may all your figs have worms! At least you *have* a family! Aunt Medusa turned everyone to stone. Half of my family is still sitting in our garden as birdbaths!" cried Alcie.

Pandy paused, a smile starting to form; she bit her lip hard to hide it.

"Maybe your dad can sell them as part of his business," she said, cleaning out her sandal.

"That's not funny!" said Alcie, breaking into a grin.

"Yes it is."

"Yes it is!" said Iole, finally joining them.

"You didn't even hear it, plebe-o!" said Alcie over her shoulder.

"Yes, well, I heard it and it's absolutely true!" said a fourth voice.

From behind a nearby cypress tree came the sound of uncontrollable laughter. Helen and Hippia, the two prettiest and most popular girls at the Athena Maiden Middle School, tumbled out of the tree's shadow.

"Well, well. Hi, maidens!" said Helen, standing straight and tossing her long blond hair back over her shoulder. "Look, Hippia . . . it's the three losers doing what they do best. Being losers. Talking about their loser families."

"Why aren't you cheerleading, Helen?" asked Pandy.

"The coach cancelled wrestling, duh. It was nailed on flyers all over school."

"So you couldn't think of anything better to do than follow us? Wow, we must be really interesting," said Alcie.

"I *so* don't think so," said Hippia. "We're going to Metis's house to plan the pre-Bacchanalia party. It's by invitation only, but I wouldn't be looking for any runners with invites if I were you."

"Oh, Hippia, don't be so mean!" said Helen. "They probably aren't even going to the Bacchanalia. So many more exciting things to do, right, guys? Like squeezing your pimples and offering up sacrifices to Aphrodite. 'Oh please, Aphrodite . . . just let me be pretty for *one* day!' Pandy, has any youth even asked you to go yet?"

Pandy stood silent, a mixture of hatred and humiliation in her brown eyes. It was true enough . . . no one had asked her. The Bacchanalia was the big school social event of the year, a ritual sacrifice, bonfire and refreshments, and then circle dancing . . . with youths! Now that she was a maiden, she didn't have to stand with the young girls off to the side; she could actually have an escort.

But not one of the young boys from the nearby Apollo Youth Academy had so much as glanced at her during intra-academy sports days. She had even smeared her neck with orange blossoms and let one strap of her toga fall ever so slightly off her shoulder when she realized she would be standing next to Tiresias the Younger during mandatory tragic chorus practice. But he just continued to sing the story of Oedipus the king: "Don't kill your father, don't marry your mother, don't poke out your eye." He didn't even notice her.

Helen sauntered up to Pandy.

"Hey, Pandy, know what everyone's saying about your dad? They say that because he's missing so much of his liver, he can't digest his food like normal people and hasn't been to the lavatorium in years. They say he's gonna blow like a volcano."

"Helen," said Pandy, "my father did something for mankind. Not like . . . oh, let me think . . . *your* father, who hid in the sewage pits during the last war."

"Take it back!"

"Helen," said Iole quietly. "Aren't you forgetting something?"

Helen whirled on Iole.

"Oh, the little dummy speaks! What, dummy?"

Iole slowly walked up to Helen.

"Pandy's father is an immortal. Which means that Pandy is a demigod. Since she became a maiden, she's started acquiring her powers. And you don't know what she can do."

Helen and Hippia looked at Pandy in silence. Pandora looked back at the two of them and tried to furrow her brow like she was going to give them flaming warts or something. Secretly, she had no idea if she even had any powers, but she wanted to give Iole a big kiss on the cheek.

Helen and Hippia started backing away.

"You'd better not try anything. My dad is on the Athens High Council," said Helen.

Alcie rummaged through her school sack. "Hey, look what I just found! A piece of my aunt Medusa. I think it's her toenail! You guys want to see it?" And she pretended to throw a piece of the Gorgon at the two retreating girls.

Helen and Hippia ran squealing for at least a hundred paces till they were out of sight.

"Nice one, Iole," said Alcie.

"Yeah, good save," said Pandy.

"I wasn't saving. You don't know what you're gonna be able to do," Iole said. "I've been reading and listening to the traveling storytellers. Demigods can be enormously powerful. Hercules is only half god and look at him! Hey, can we take a walk through the market? My mom gave me some extra drachmas to buy figs on the way home."

The three girls turned from the chariot road, climbed up a gentle slope to another low wall, scrambled over, and entered the *agora,* the main Athens marketplace.

Pandy loved the marketplace and wished she didn't

usually have to hurry home to help babysit. She could stroll (these days, it was more like disappear) for hours among the brilliantly woven tapestries from Persia, glass jars filled with beads from Namibia and rare spices from China, and baskets of dried Macedonian figs, Turkish apricots, and Arabian dates.

"How are my favorite girls?" said the fruit vendor, when they entered his stall. "Why haven't you troublemakers been to see me lately?"

"Hi, Glaucus," said the girls in unison.

"We've been inundated with this huge school project; pretty much working on it every day. Well, some of us have," said Iole, specifically not glancing at Pandy.

"Ah, yes," said Glaucus, "the big Gods' project. A few maidens have been in buying dried grapes, apples, and whatnot. Making big dioramas and mini battle scenes, sticking things up on papyrus boards, making little gods-on-a-stick."

"With *fruit*?" said Alcie.

"Some kids were very creative," said Glaucus.

"I'm toast!" whispered Pandy to Alcie. "If I don't at least get a passing mark on this project, I'll get held back a whole year. I'd be the only maiden in a class full of little girls! I'd rather be sent to the underworld. Gods, I can't think about this right now, come on!"

While Iole wasted long minutes choosing just the right figs, Pandy drew Alcie to the vendor with rainbows of colored silk fluttering above his stall; the girls walked among bolts of gauze, linen, and cotton piled high all over his stand. Pandy imagined herself dressed in beautiful togas made of these fabrics, each one more dazzling than the last. She wondered what color Tiresias the Younger liked.

"All right, I'm done," said Iole, joining them. "Let's go."

A few minutes later they reached the crossroad that led to their homes.

"Hey, why don't you guys come over?" said Pandy. "You can help me figure out what I'm gonna bring tomorrow."

"And help you babysit? I don't think so, thank you very much," said Alcie. "I have geometry and civics homework."

"I have to help my dad feed the animals," said Iole. "Catallus, our stable slave, just got his results back from his session with our seer and it turns out he's got Castor's Contagious Cough, so he's living in the toolshed now and we're a little shorthanded."

"Okay . . . I'll see you guys tomorrow."

The three friends started to walk away.

"Pandy!" called Alcie.

"What?"

"I'm sorry, too."

Pandy turned and waved. They waved back and disappeared over a crest.

She felt something cool and wet touch her knee. Dido, her shepherd dog, was at her heels, meeting her as he did every day when she returned home from school. She bent down and put her arms around his thick neck. No matter how disastrously, devastatingly crushing her life was, Dido had never disappointed her.

"Hey, Dido. How are you, huh? You big ghost dog."

She called him that because Dido was white. Ghost white. His fur, skin, nose, eyes, everything about Dido was the color of snow. Only a small circle of pure blue around the iris with a tiny dot of black in the middle of each eye let her know where Dido was looking at any moment. He licked her face with his big white tongue, and trotted on ahead of her toward the house.

She followed him, certain in her heart that the rest of her days would be crushing, horrible, and devastating, just like this one.

CHAPTER TWO

At Home

Pandy's house sat on top of a small hill in a quiet Athens suburb. Her father had built it from his own design, and it was modest but spacious, with a large front courtyard surrounded by a stone wall. From her sleeping room upstairs, she could see right across the whole valley, and could just make out the edges of the agora and the top of the new Parthenon.

Turning into her courtyard, she spotted half a dozen dryads, tiny multiwinged moss green tree nymphs busily knocking the heads off of her mother's narcissus blossoms. One was eating single bites out of every vegetable in the garden and promptly spitting them out. Another was building a small fortress out of artichoke leaves and still another was painting a rude fresco of Pandy's entire family standing on their heads under the words "Dryads WAS here!" in blue cloudberry juice on the courtyard wall.

"Scat!" Pandy yelled.

Dido raced amongst them, scattering the tiny creatures, who shook their fists at the snarling white furball, swearing as they fled that they would be back.

Inside, the house was still. Pandy headed for the food cupboards. There was a note nailed to a shelf just above the olive jars.

Pandora,
The tooth physician sent a runner; he's overbooked today and wants to see you tomorrow instead. Your mom is working late at Zeus's temple. I'm installing an atrium in the city and should be back by six. Sabina is watching your brother. Try to play with him just a little. Thanks.
Lots and lots of phileo,
Daddy

Well, at least she didn't have to see the tooth physician, but Gods, now she had to play with Xander. It wasn't that she didn't love Xander, she just didn't like him. Well, she could sorta tolerate most things about him, but there was one thing she just couldn't stand anymore: his tail. It was a stubby nubbin when he'd been an infant, so no one knew exactly what kind of a tail it was, but as he grew older it was obvious that Xander, only son of the House of Prometheus, was part peacock.

Pandy remembered creeping down the hall late at

night, listening to her parents speaking in their room just after he was born; her dad whispering and yelling at the same time and her mother, Sybilline, saying she simply didn't know *how* it happened.

"Well I'll tell you *how* it happened," Prometheus had said. "You scrimped . . . and you know you did, Syb . . . on your offering to Hera the *day* before Xander was born. What were you thinking? The most vicious and vindictive of all the immortals and you take chicken eggs, not the quail eggs she prefers, to Hera's temple. And now our son has a tail!"

Hera, Queen of the Gods, had two symbols, two animals that she protected, the cow and the peacock.

"Worry and complain, worry and complain," Sybilline said calmly. "I choose to believe that the boy is clearly going to be a favorite of Hera's."

"I'm just thankful he doesn't have an udder," Prometheus mumbled.

Funny thing was, Pandy could remember actually liking her little brother at one time, tail and all. But now his constant three-year-old laughter, energy, and need for his big sister just wore on her like an ox yoke.

Pandy grabbed a handful of dried grapes and headed upstairs, pausing on the stairway just long enough to bow to the small statue of Athena sitting in her altar niche.

She knew she could just slip by her brother's room

without even looking in. He probably wouldn't see her and she could get right to her homework, but she poked her head in anyway. Empty. His stuffed animal skins were untouched on his little sleeping pallet. Suddenly, Pandy heard a squeal coming from her parents' room.

Tossing her book sack into her own room as she passed, she pulled aside her parents' filmy red privacy curtain and saw Xander and the old house-slave, Sabina, playing on the floor with something shiny. Sabina's white hair was pinned back in a style Pandy only saw painted on antique ceramic urns, and her skin was so thin it was glimmering, almost translucent, even in the darkened sleeping room.

Sabina had been with the family since before Pandy had been born, but she never knew exactly where Sabina had come from. Her mother had told her Sabina used to be a cook or something, which made Pandy laugh since Sabina couldn't even dip a piece of bread in olive oil and make it taste good. All Prometheus would say was that Sabina had done a wonderful job helping to raise Pandy and that she was a fine woman, period.

But through the years, with her growing curiosity propelling her toward drawn curtains and listening to whispered conversations, Pandy had come to know the truth.

Sabina was a Fate.

The lost Fate. The hapless Fate. The Fate nobody talked about.

Pandy knew all about the Fates: three immortal sisters, old as the stars, who sat around a huge spinning wheel and plotted the course of every person's life. Clotho, the Spinner, would spin out a thread every time someone was born. Lachesis, the Disposer of Lots, would assign their destiny; a stable boy here, a hero there. And Atropos, the most feared of all, was the Fate who cut the thread when someone was supposed to die.

But there was a fourth Fate. A younger sister who, from the first, was just a little too scattered and unfocused for proper "fating." Her sisters had tried putting her at the spinning wheel, but the thread she spun was very lumpy, and she created a whole series of people who weighed over five hundred pounds. When she tried to assign destinies she felt sorry for everyone and created a world of happy heroes with nothing to do. Finally, they gave Sabina the "abhorred shears," but she kept getting distracted and not cutting the thread in time, letting hundreds of people live past the age of 250.

Since there was obviously no place for Sabina around the wheel, her sisters sent her to Mount Olympus and Zeus put her to work in the kitchen. But she wasn't any good there either and the food of the gods, nectar and ambrosia, would arrive either too hot, too cold, or too late at Zeus's table. The only time that Sabina seemed to be really happy was when she was with children. So, when the Great House of Prometheus was expecting a little girl, Zeus sent Sabina to earth to help out with Pandy.

But now that Pandy was older, Sabina spent most of her time doing the thing she loved most: playing with Xander.

Pandy flattened herself against the entryway, trying not to make a sound.

Good, Pandy thought, Sabina has everything under control and I am *so* not necessary here. She tiptoed past the curtain and slipped into her own room.

Kicking off her sandals, she sat down on her sleeping pallet, examining the bruise left on her heel by the rock earlier. It was small, no big deal. But she rubbed it stubbornly until it actually started to hurt. She took off the training girdle for her toga. She'd seen beautiful girdles on other girls, cinching in their togas at the waist, making their figures look slim. But hers was small and leather and stupid. She was a maiden now, so why couldn't she wear a large, silver girdle like her mother?

She thought of her mother, sitting behind her desk at Zeus's Athens temple . . . or as Pandy called it, "Supreme Ruler, Inc., Athens Branch." Why Zeus had hired her mother was another thing that was totally beyond her understanding. Sure, her mother could organize things and her handwriting was nice, but she wasn't very easy to talk to. Not lately anyway. Maybe, as Zeus's chief personal aide, her mother didn't have to say anything; maybe she just filed stuff and took messages for the temple's high priestess.

That thought brought her back to her long overdue assignment: what to bring for the school project. She knew that some classes had actually worked together on their presentations, but her teacher had allowed everyone in her class to "do their own thing."

What would illustrate the enduring presence of the great gods of Greece in her life? She considered taking the statue of Athena from its niche in the stairwell, but it was heavy and every home had one of Athena or one of the other great gods, nothing special there. She could take one of her mother's many paycheck presents from Zeus: golden bracelets, silver toga clasps, hairpins of mother-of-pearl. But as Zeus liked to employ many, many women at his various temples, these were also common throughout Athens.

Perhaps if she had a small nap, she thought, she'd have more energy to think of something. Her room was chilled; the embers in her grate were stone cold from the morning fire.

Time for the trick. The trick her father had taught her when she was very small and made her promise not to show anyone else. "Not everyone can do this, Pandora, and we don't want people getting resentful." So she'd kept it to herself, but she didn't think it was anything special.

She knelt down by the grate and blew gently on the dark ashes. Only a few seconds later a thin wisp of smoke began to drift up and the larger cinders glowed a dull red. She kept blowing until the dull red color became bright, bright orange and the ashes started giving off a soothing warmth.

She lay back down, the heat now circling around her. She closed her eyes and . . . oh, her pallet was so comfy. Maybe she could pluck a tail feather from her brother for the project, she thought, as she drifted off. Would only hurt him for a second . . . and if no one was around to see it . . .

And she was fast asleep.

She woke a few hours later and realized the house was silent. Groggy, she clomped to her parents' room to check on her brother. She parted the curtain and saw Sabina, fast asleep and snoring, on her parents' day pallet, her hand still clutching the shiny object. It was her mother's favorite Zeus present, a gold bangle with three large emeralds in it. Her mother would be furious if she knew Xander had been allowed to play with it, so Pandy gingerly pried it out of Sabina's gnarled hand. Then she realized her baby brother was nowhere to be seen.

Okay, she thought, she would casually put the bracelet back first and *then* panic. She knelt down beside her parents' sleeping pallet, which was raised a good meter off the floor. Reaching underneath for the box where her mother kept Zeus's gifts, her fingers touched the top of a tiny feathered rump. She shrieked and pulled her hand back. Xander, laughing uproariously, crawled out from under the pallet, his mother's pearl earrings hanging from his mouth.

Oh fine, she thought, my little brother could have choked and somehow, some way, everyone would have blamed it on me.

"Come on you little satyr, give those to me!" she said.

"No!" he giggled over the earrings and retreated under the bed.

"Xander! Give those to me right now!"

She started to crawl in after him and, grabbing hold of one of his chubby legs, pulled him back close to her. He squealed with delight and kicked her square in the forehead, dropping the pearls.

"Ahh! You little goat!"

She watched Xander's tiny legs dash around the pallet and out of her parents' room. A moment later, he was gleefully throwing stuffed skins around in his own room. Pandy heard Sabina gnashing her teeth as the old woman shifted position.

Gods, she thought, Hades could drive his chariot out of the underworld right now and Sabina wouldn't wake up.

Pandy reached for the earrings and looked around for her mother's jewelry box. Xander had pushed it back against the far wall, behind a pile of small rolled floor rugs that her mother kept stored for "good company." Pandy pushed the rugs aside . . . and felt something underneath. Thrusting her hand into the rolls, she scratched it on a metal edge.

"Ow!"

Feeling along its shape, she pulled out an odd metal case with a small bronze lock.

The lid was made of gold with faint streaks of a white and red metal blended in. The sides and back were of black onyx, blue lapis, and pink marble, each length intricately carved to depict scenes of the family. On one side, her mother was shown reclining on a sofa. On the back, Pandy saw herself as a much younger girl, walking with her parents in an olive grove. Her father and mother were shown on another side facing each other in profile, smiling. There was something familiar about it, but she couldn't think what it was. Curiosity began to rise up inside her like cream left too long to boil, and suddenly all she knew was that she really, really wanted to look inside.

But the old lock was thick and she couldn't get it to release just by shaking or tugging on it. Her fingernails weren't long enough (because she kept biting them) to pick it, so she crawled back to her mother's jewel case and found a straight silver hairpin. She pushed and jiggled and wedged the end of the pin into the bottom of the lock. At first it refused to release, but finally the lock started to give, and the clasp released with a tiny click.

Lifting the lid slowly, Pandy made out the shape of another smaller box inside: plain dark wood, very simple with slight curves at each of its corners. She brought it out from under the pallet and into the fading afternoon sunlight.

"Gods," she said softly.

This box she remembered. She hadn't seen it in so many moons she couldn't even recollect the last time; but she knew instantly what it was and what was inside.

Pandy set it down gently on the pallet. The wood was old but smooth; the hinges and clasp made of adamant, the same metal that had once chained her father to a rock as punishment for giving fire to mankind, a metal only Hercules could break. But there was no lock on the clasp, only a large circle of red wax stamped with the great seal of Zeus.

She shivered. "They" were all still in there. She even imagined she saw the box jiggle a little, as if what was inside was trying to get out.

Her father didn't often tell this part of his story and when he did, it was usually late at night, after a few glasses of wine. His voice would drop so low that Pandy would have trouble eavesdropping from the staircase, but she knew he was reliving the moment when Zeus had entrusted the box to him, to be kept a secret forever.

After Prometheus had brought it back home and hidden it away, he'd forgotten it was even in his keeping most of the time. But Pandy remembered first finding it when she was six and running carelessly through the house with it. She had never seen her father so scared. When he finally caught up with her, he grabbed the box and started to shake her hard. It was only after she started to sob did he stop and hold her close for so long that she thought she would stop breathing.

Prometheus sat her down and after a long moment he turned to her. He slowly explained to her, in terms he struggled to make her understand, that she must never, ever touch the box. What was inside, if it ever got out, would make mankind very, very sad.

"I promise, Daddy."

"Good girl, Pandora. Now, go . . . play outside, or something," he said.

"With what?" she asked.

"I don't know. With the goat. With anything."

At the entryway, she watched him slowly get up, still trembling, and take the box back upstairs.

Over the years, Pandy had come to know, by listening in the stairwell when she should have been asleep, the exact story of why the box was so important and why her father decided that simply storing the thing underneath a pile of rugs wasn't precaution enough. He'd had a strong metal case and lock forged to keep it safe.

What she didn't know was that since then he had looked in the case so many times simply to reassure himself, that the lock had become weak and simple to break . . . with a straight silver hairpin.

All the evils of the world were in this box.

Pandy shook it.

It really didn't look all that terrifying.

And then, the idea flew into her head.

What if she took the box to school for the big project?

Of course, she wouldn't open it.

Duh.

No, there was no way . . . what if she dropped it? Or accidentally left it in her school cupboard? Or left it in the sun and the great seal started to melt?

She looked at the box again. It was a *neato* example of the gods' enduring presence and nobody—*nobody*— would have anything else like it. She would be so careful. She would wrap it in a large sheet of papyrus, or a pallet linen or something, and tie it tightly with a strand of strong hemp.

"Gods!" she whispered. "I might even get an alpha on the project! And that would bring my overall grade up to beta!"

She looked at Sabina, still snoring.

Pandy clasped the box tight, careful not to touch the

seal, and carried it into her room. She was placing it under her pallet when she heard her father downstairs. She stood up fast, her breath caught in her throat.

"Pandora!" he called. "Honey, your mom's not home yet, so come help me with the evening meal."

Shaking off a twinge of shame, she called back, "Okay, Dad . . . what are we having?"

"Leftover sacrificial lamb and rice. I'm getting the fire started now."

Pandy visualized the tip of his right forefinger glowing orange as it always did when he touched the dried kindling twigs.

She walked out into the hallway. Sabina was stumbling out from her parents' room.

"Whazz happen? Wherz yer baby brothuh?" she slurred, still sleepy.

"Oh, he fell down the stairs and broke his arm, but it's okay because Apollo stopped by and fixed it so he's fine now. Go back to sleep."

"Wha . . . ?"

"I'm kidding, Sabina. He's in his room."

Leaving the old woman speechless, Pandy went downstairs.

CHAPTER THREE
Dear Diary

That night, Pandy spent a long time on her hands and knees staring at the box under her pallet. She had no idea what she expected to see, but she now wanted almost any excuse not to take the thing to school. There was a strange pressure, like a soft ache, in her stomach. Dido, curled up by the fire grate, occasionally opened one white eye to gaze at his mistress.

Finally Pandy stood up, took off her school toga, and put on her sleeping garments. Now that she was a maiden, she was beginning to detest her combed cotton night-robes with the face of Iris, Goddess of the Rainbow, and the little multicolored arches splashed all over them. She pulled her lavender-colored privacy curtain closed and moved her footstool to the base of her tall wooden shelves and, reaching up high, pulled down a small brown wolfskin; the head with its two huge ears still attached.

"Come on, Dido, move," she said, walking to the fire grate and nudging him with her foot. "You can lay down again once it's on the floor."

Dido padded off a few meters to wait while Pandy spread the wolfskin in front of the grate. Pandy lay down on top of it with her face close to the wolf head and beckoned to Dido, then she closed her eyes.

"Dear Diary," she said quietly into one of the wolf ears.

The dark, lifeless eyes of the wolf flared with a greenish yellow spark. This was a diary unlike any other, a present to Pandy on her eighth birthday from Artemis, Goddess of the Moon and lover of wild things. Other girls had common diaries made of papyrus pages, needing India ink. But because of Artemis's great affection for her friend Prometheus, his daughter Pandy had a diary that talked to her.

"Blessed you are among mortals. Good evening, Pandora. What do you have to tell me?" said the wolf head, its voice soft and high, yet . . . crunchy. Like someone walking on a pile of rough pebbles.

"Oh . . . nothing much." She hesitated. "I saw a boy I liked today . . ."

"The same one you told me about two weeks ago?" said the wolf.

"Yes . . . Tiresias the Younger."

"Fine. Just keeping track. Go on."

"Yeah. Well, that's about all. Oh, Helen and Hippia were ragging on Dad again today. Iole said that they'd better be careful because I'm probably getting my powers or something and I have no idea what powers she's talking about. Do you know anything about—"

"Pandora, we've been through this before: I record what you say only as a source of reference and remembrance. I will tell you everything you've ever done, or said, or thought, provided you told me, but I cannot advise you regarding what is to come."

"Yeah, yeah . . . *fine*," Pandy said.

"Oh, we're in a mood tonight, are we? I don't think that tone is actually necessary, Pandora," said the wolf.

"Okay . . . well then, that's about it."

"Really?"

"Yes."

"Very good then," the skin said.

Pandy paused.

"Why?" she asked.

"Nothing," said the wolf.

"No, what?"

"I just thought you might want to tell me about that thing under the pallet."

"What thing? I don't . . ."

"Pandora! Shall I take you back to that day when you told me, 'Today is the day I stop lying forever'? I've got that entry right on the tip of my tongue, little one. Besides,

I can see the thing from here. I won't ask you, but if you want to tell me, I'm all ears."

"It's just a box." Pandy tried to sound casual. "A box that Zeus gave Dad. And I'm just gonna take it to school tomorrow and show it off and . . . and . . . that's it. No biggie."

There was a long pause.

"I see," said the wolf. "Curiosity killed the Caledonian Boar, you know."

"Yeah . . . huh?"

There was a long, long silence.

"Is that all, Pandora?"

"Yes," Pandy muttered, "that's all. Except if Dido has anything to tell me."

Dido immediately opened his eyes and stared straight at the wolf, whining softly and every so often glancing at Pandy. After about two minutes, during which the wolf mumbled things like "Oh!" and "Uh-huh," Dido put his head down again and closed his eyes.

"Pandora," said the wolf. "Dido is fine. But he asks that you let him sleep on the end of your pallet tonight because he's a little chilled, that you put a little more meat and not so many entrails in his food bowl, and that you stop *lying*!"

"Yeah, okay . . . okay . . . wait, *what*?"

"Good night, daughter of Prometheus. Sleep well in the arms of Morpheus. Blessed are you among mortals."

And with that, the wolf head was silent.

"I'm not lying. I'm *not*," Pandy said.

Pandy got to her feet, rolled the skin up, and placed it back on the shelf. After using her tooth-rake, she climbed in between the pallet linens. She turned onto her side only to find Dido, wide-awake and staring her in the face.

"Oh, okay, c'mon," she said.

Dido immediately jumped onto the end of her pallet, turned around three times, and settled down.

Pandy just lay there with her arms folded across her chest.

"And I don't lie."

Dido, almost asleep, gave a teeny little snort.

CHAPTER FOUR
School

The next morning, Pandy had a vague feeling that her dreams had all been miserable, and she was thankful she couldn't really remember them. She stood in front of her fire grate for a bit, then dressed in her undergarments and put on her plain brown cotton-linen school toga. She studied herself in her looking glass. The pimple that was on its way to the size of a volcano only the day before had thankfully decided not to poke out of her nose, and now it was just a tiny red dot, but the kick from Xander had turned into a nice purple bruise on her forehead.

She looked at her brown eyes, which she hated because they weren't blue, and straight brown hair, which she hated because it wasn't curly, and her teeth, which she hated because of her slight overbite.

"Great Aphrodite," she whispered, "just let me be pretty for one day."

She thought of Helen and Hippia, and how the youths went out of their way to walk close to them and leave narcissus blossoms in their paths. She couldn't understand how the gods could bestow so many favors on the two meanest girls in school.

Sabina called from below.

"First meal!"

"Be right there."

She fastened her hair back off her face with a tortoise-shell pin, one of her "You're a Maiden Now!" presents from her parents.

Coming downstairs, she saw her father at the drainage counter, packing her school meal as usual, while Sabina stood next to him sniffing vegetables for the evening meal.

Her mother sat at the table, teasing her little brother with spoonfuls of creamed oats as she tried to get him to eat.

"Where does the Nemean Lion live? Huh? Come on honey, open up. Just one bite for Mother? Where does he live? In his caaave!"

Sybilline wore another new bracelet on her wrist; Zeus had obviously been very generous with her pay the day before. It was twisted silver with a yellow stone the size of an olive sitting in the middle, and it made Sybilline's wrist and fingers look all the more perfectly sculpted. Her mother actually could have been a statue, Pandy thought. Her hair, the color of gold coins, with never a curl out of place; her aquiline nose and almond-shaped eyes were subjects of discussion in market stalls whenever Sybilline went shopping. But it was her skin that was really perfect: porcelain smooth with not a freckle or hint of a wrinkle. Pandy had lost count of the times she'd gazed at her own reflection, trying to pray away the sprinkling of freckles across her nose and cheeks.

"Apollo-dots," her dad had said, catching her crying over her looking glass one night. "It just means that the Sun-God loves you more than most."

Pandy didn't believe it. She thought her mother had made some sort of deal with the "god of ugliness" (although she knew no such god existed) to give her the most hideous daughter ever so everyone would always find Sybilline more beautiful.

"Good morning, daughter," Sybilline said.

Pandy bowed. "Morning, Mother."

"Just a moment, Pandora," her mother said, stopping her short. "What's that on your face?"

"It's just a bruise. Xander and I were playing . . ."

"No, my dear, not that." Sybilline pointed to Pandy's nose. "That!"

Pandy felt the remnants of the pimple, even smaller than before.

"Oh, my dear," her mother sighed, "I just wish that once in your life you would listen to me. A little dab of goat's urine on those things and, *poof,* gone!"

"Muuuther . . ."

Pandy hated this.

"Sabina, would you please finish feeding Xander? I just can't get him to eat. You know, honey, I was talking to Helen's and Hippia's mothers yesterday and those girls are doing so nicely. Straight-alpha students and cheerleaders. So well adjusted. And you could be just like them, Pandora, if you could just be a little more . . ."

"Syb," Pandy's father called from the drainage counter.

"Well, it's true, darling," Sybilline said, cupping Pandy's face with her free hand as she handed Sabina the feeding spoon. "You have such nice features, my sweet plum, if only you wouldn't hide them. Maybe some irons for your hair, hmm? Perhaps a little more exercise and you could lose . . ."

"Her hair's fine, Syb," Prometheus said as Pandy slumped away from her mother.

"Hi, Dad," she said, standing on her toes as he bent down to receive her kiss. Pandy remembered a time when her father was stronger and more athletic, chasing her amongst the cypress trees during family picnics or harnessing the stallions to their chariot. Now, after years of owning his own in-home atrium construction business and dealing with all the hassles, his sturdy frame had a few less muscles and a few more wrinkles and sags.

"Hi, honey."

"What's for mid-meal?" she asked, and then said right along with him, "Stuffed grape leaves, flat bread, dried goat, olives, and oatie cakes."

"Well, sweetie, if you want to make your own mid-meal . . ."

"It's fine, Dad. Thanks," said Pandy, grinning.

She bumped him playfully, nestling in close, loving the way he smelled of leather and cedar oil. She saw for the first time that his jet-black hair was graying a bit at the sides and his brown eyes had a slightly tired quality to them.

"Want a bowl of creamed oats?"

"Nah. Not really hungry. Just some of these," she said, dipping her hand into the date jar.

"What are you bringing for your big school project, honey? It's due today, right?" asked Prometheus.

Pandy froze, jolted out of their momentary closeness. How did he know about the project? How did her parents always know everything? Half the time they didn't care about her at all and the other half they were asking about stuff she'd just as soon they forgot about.

She didn't want to lie to her father (she remembered what her diary had said and she wanted to kick it);

lately she'd taken to sort of grunting yes or no to any of his questions. But there was no way of getting out of this.

"Um . . . haven't really decided yet," she replied. It was kinda true, she thought: if she found anything better than a box containing all of man's misery, sealed by Zeus himself, she'd take it.

"I might bring some roasted corn," she said, thinking fast. "Add a little water and let it bake in the sun and use it to demonstrate how Demeter, the great Goddess of the Harvest, keeps us well fed. That would show how . . . they . . . the gods . . . um . . . influence . . . us . . . now."

She looked at her dad to see if her explanation had worked.

"Well," he said, tightening the hemp string on her food sack, "it sounds . . . good. But after two months, I expected a bit more from you, daughter."

"A *bit* more?" said Sybilline, wiping creamed oats off of her perfect fingers. "Gods, Pandora, with all of the gifts I've been given, you could take the simplest bangle and say the gods are present in our everyday lives because they are giving me . . . I mean us . . . well, your father and me at any rate, riches for our old age!"

No one said anything.

"Oh, never mind. The steeds of Apollo are galloping around my brain. I have to rid myself of this headache before work this afternoon. I'm off to the bath," she said, rising gracefully, one hand to her forehead. "Good luck, my daughter."

Sybilline bent slightly to not quite kiss the top of Pandy's head, then drifted upstairs.

"There was a happy hour celebration at the temple yesterday," Prometheus said after a moment. "Your mother had a little too much wine."

"Guess so. Okay, well thanks for mid-meal, Dad. See you later."

Pandy grabbed the sack and headed for the staircase.

"Hey, silly! The academy's that way!" Prometheus said, pointing out the door.

"Right," said Pandy, sagging a bit. All this deceit was making her slightly nauseated. "I just forgot my track sandals. Be right back."

In her room, she unloaded her mid-meal sack and put the food into her soiled-toga basket. Then she reached underneath her sleeping pallet and pulled out the wooden box. Wrapping it in one of her silk festival veils, she hurriedly stuffed it into her sack and retied the hemp string. She found an old hair ribbon and wrapped it fast around the hemp. Finally, she stuck one of her hairpins through the neck of the sack.

She suddenly felt exactly the way she always did when she was doing something she knew no one would like: tired, heavy around the middle, and kinda angry.

She was almost out of her room when she remembered her track sandals. Throwing them over her shoulder, she went back downstairs and headed for the door.

"Um, excuse me, Pandora?" said her father.

She jumped.

"What? Oh, sorry, Dad. Um, what?"

"Where's your school supply sack?"

"Don't need to bring it today, Dad. Classes have been cancelled because of the Gods project."

"Well then, how about a kiss for your old father?"

"Oh . . . sure." She lifted her head up to his bearded cheek and gave him a big kiss. Before she turned to go, she hugged his waist tightly.

"I love you, Dad. Big-time phileo."

"Me you more, my daughter," he said.

Pandy ran off to school, feeling like her uncle Atlas: pretty much carrying the weight of the heavens.

The Athena Maiden Middle School was set in a large cypress grove just outside the main city walls. The city had only recently decreed that girls and maidens would be allowed to receive an education, so the buildings and the outdoor teaching groves were new and well kept. The school was very progressive, offering track-and-field classes, math and the known sciences, philosophy, and gourmet cooking. At the heart of the school was the outdoor amphitheater: a huge semicircle of rows and rows of benches set into a steeply sloping hillside. Up to six hundred students at once could watch plays or hear lectures from visiting poets, storytellers, and great thinkers standing on the stage far below. Because of the amphitheater's cone shape, even the slightest whisper onstage could be heard in the top row of seats. There was a rumor the amphitheater was actually built on top of a recently extinct volcano, which was why they could hold winter classes there with the underground heat keeping everybody warm.

Arriving late, Pandy saw Alcie and Iole among a large crowd of students heading off toward the amphitheater.

She threw her sandals in her school cupboard and, holding tight to the sack, dashed off to catch up.

"Hey," Pandy said, finally reaching them through the crowd.

"We were starting to get worried," said Iole.

"What did you finally decide to bring?" asked Alcie.

"You'll see. It's cool."

"You're not even going to tell us? You're going to lump us in with all the other plebe-os and clayheads around here?" asked Alcie.

"Yep."

"Not even a hint?" asked Iole.

"Nope."

"Fine," Alcie replied. "Then you don't get to see my dad's toes until everyone else does."

"Whatever. Hey, Iole, what's on your cheek?" asked Pandy.

Iole had painted, in yellow clay, an almost-perfect reproduction of a large fingerprint on her right cheek.

"Just a small illustration. In case anyone wants to know exactly where Apollo healed me."

Alcie and Pandy just looked at each other, taking their seats along with hundreds of other girls and maidens.

For the next few hours, the entire academy watched as students demonstrated the theme of the project.

There were weapons of all kinds brought by students whose fathers claimed to have been given them by Ares.

Several girls brought jars of foul-smelling beauty creams, unguents, and lotions their mothers swore were presents from Aphrodite herself.

One entire class acted out the scene of Athena giving the olive tree to Athens, thereby becoming the city's patron goddess. Both Helen and Hippia had demanded to play Athena so forcefully that now both girls stood onstage, alternating Athena's lines and occasionally shoving each other out of the way.

Some girls had written poems, others had composed songs. One older girl even trotted out her two-headed calf, claiming that Hera had obviously blessed the family.

"Yeah," whispered Alcie out of the corner of her mouth, "same amount of milk, twice the feed. Big blessing."

Finally, Master Epeus's class took the stage.

Iole followed after a girl who put on a rather elaborate puppet show: "Why We Have Winter." Pandy and Alcie were worried about the reception Iole might get with her sad little fingerprint, but in a clear voice that seemed too big for her small body, Iole told the tale of her illness, her mother's fervent prayers, and Apollo's healing touch. Her story was so simple and poignant that, not only was there a hush throughout the amphitheater, even the birds and squirrels were absolutely silent.

When Iole finished, Pandy noticed most of the students and a few of the teachers had tears in their eyes. The applause began as Iole started to walk offstage until it built into a roar that lasted several minutes.

"That was really great, Iole," said Pandy, as her friend slid back into her seat.

"Nice going," said Alcie. "Okay, I'm up."

Alcie walked onto the stage carrying a small blue silk pouch. Reaching inside, she withdrew an apparatus that looked like four blanched almonds on a thin string. She held it high for everyone to see.

"These are my father's toes!"

After the first collective groan, a few students started to giggle. As Alcie strode around, shaking the toes over her head and retelling the story of how her father lost the originals and had these wooden toes made, everyone joined in laughing. Then, when she said that she could always tell when he didn't have his sandals on because of the tapping sound he made, the laughter built to the point that Alcie didn't even have to open her mouth. She finally just stood there, sporadically shaking the string of toes over her head, and the students fell all over themselves in hysterics.

Iole was wiping away the tears from her eyes as Alcie rejoined them.

"My sides hurt. I can't walk," she panted.

"Yeah, well neither can my dad," said Alcie.

Pandy had been too nervous to really laugh. During Alcie's speech, she'd been untying the ribbon and hemp strand. Now she held the sack tightly in both hands.

"Here I go."

She walked up the steps and out into the middle of the stage, the sack held behind her, and turned to face the crowd.

Immediately she caught the eye of Master Epeus, who furrowed his brows, already disappointed, and pointed down to his toenails.

Some of the girls were still laughing at Alcie, but when Pandy didn't speak for a few seconds, they quieted down.

"My name is Pandora Atheneus Andromaeche Helena, daughter of the House . . . the *Great* House of Prometheus."

She heard a few whispers and a loud hoot. She knew what they were expecting.

"You all know the story," she plunged on, "of how my father stole fire from the Sky-Lord Zeus, and brought it down to earth so mankind could be warm and safe. And you know that Zeus punished him by letting a great eagle eat his liver each day and having it grow back each night."

"Here we go," moaned a maiden in the front row.

Pandy looked at the crowd of girls, whispering among themselves, not paying any attention. Some were getting up and wandering off. Even the teachers looked bored.

"But there was a second part to his punishment that you do not know about. Something that my father never talks about because it is so terrible that many of you will . . . faint. And because that's just my dad."

Several girls stopped whispering.

"Besides my dad's liver in a jar, which I did not bring, Zeus gave my father a box containing"—she paused—"all of the misery of the world."

The teachers began staring at her strangely.

"Each of the great Olympians put something really bad into the box and they gave it to my dad for safekeeping. If the box is ever opened, plagues of every kind will . . . will . . . fly out and torment each of you for the rest of your lives. Your skin will bubble. Your hair will fall out. Wild beasts will eat you in your sleep. It will hail every day and there will be lots of floods. And there will be nothing you can do but cry and beseech the gods. Nothing!"

In one swift motion she brought the sack out from behind her back, withdrew the box, and lifted it high over her head.

"And they're all in here!"

CHAPTER FIVE

Uh-Oh

There was a deathly silence in the amphitheater.

Pandy, feeling just a little bolder now that she had their attention, slowly walked to a small stairway at the other side of the stage.

"Some of you might not believe me," Pandy went on, descending the stairs. "It's a very simple box."

She walked up to some terrified girls in the front row.

"It doesn't really look all that important."

She impulsively thrust the box right in the face of Brynhild, the Viking exchange student who constantly beat her up during wrestling. Brynhild shrieked and fell backward off her bench.

"But *here* . . . ," Pandy said, pointing at the blob of hard red wax, "is the great seal of Zeus himself, with *his* thunderbolt!"

She walked back up the stairs and onto the stage, but

not before frightening a few more students by shoving the box under their noses.

"I brought this to show you that, even though you all pretty much take fire for granted now, my dad—my whole family—is constantly living with the presence of the gods. And we . . . all of us, but mostly my dad . . . are saving you guys every day from a fate worse than death!"

She stopped. Hundreds of terrified eyes stared back at her.

"Thank you very much."

Holding the box tightly, she walked off the stage in silence.

Alcie and Iole met her as she descended the steps.

"Are you kidding with that?" said Alcie, her eyebrows knitted into one long line.

"No."

Iole stared at Pandy, her face drained of almost all color.

"You took an awful chance bringing it to school."

"It's no big deal," Pandy said replacing the box in the sack. "Look . . . all gone!"

But she was shaking hard as she started to walk away.

"Where are you going?" said Alcie.

"I have to get this home."

"Fine, we'll come with you," Alcie replied.

They walked back along the portico to get Pandy's track sandals, and were almost to her cupboard when Helen and Hippia appeared from behind a column.

"Hey, Pandy!" said Helen. "Pretty neat trick. Fooling everyone like that," she said.

"What?"

"You don't really expect anyone to believe that everything bad is in that little box, do you? Everyone is talking about what a stupid joke that was and what a loser you are," said Hippia.

"I think I overheard Master Epeus say he wished he could give you something lower than a delta. Maybe an omega," said Helen.

"Well, that's too bad and I don't really care . . ."

"Let me see it," said Helen.

"As if!" said Alcie.

"Come on . . . just for a sec," said Hippia.

"Look, I know you two are insane, but there's no way . . . ," said Iole.

"Shut up, dummy! Come on, Pandy, please?" said Hippia.

"No way."

Pandy turned toward her cupboard feeling like she'd just won a battle. At long last she had something that these girls wanted!

"Pandy . . . ," Helen said in a honeyed voice. "Hippia

and I weren't very nice to you yesterday, about the pre-Bacchanalia party and everything. We think it might be fun if you were there. And we were talking to Tiresias the Younger. He thinks you're very cute, and his date's come down with some sort of pox so he doesn't have anyone to go with."

"So," continued Hippia, "let us look at the box, and we'll arrange the whole thing."

Pandy turned, about to tell them exactly what part of Hades they could go to when Helen said,

"Your friends can come, too."

Gods!

Gods, if it were only her, she would have walked away. But now Alcie and Iole were part of it. Pandy was no fool. The three of them really didn't have many other friends and most girls thought the trio was very odd. *Losers* and *plebes* were the words everyone used. This was not only her chance to get in with the popular girls, but it was Alcie's and Iole's as well. She looked at Iole, who stared hard back at her as if to say, "Don't even think about it." But Pandy saw a glimmer of excitement pass over Alcie's eyes, even though Alcie was trying her very best to look like she couldn't care less. It was an opportunity for all three of them to be something other than losers, something other than themselves.

"Fine," she said at last, "but be careful and don't touch the seal."

"Pandy!" shrieked Iole.

"It's okay, dummy, we won't do anything to it," said Hippia.

Pandy reached into the sack, withdrew the box, and extended it to Helen, but her arm suddenly felt as if it were made of lead. And the ache was back in her stomach.

Iole threw herself between Pandy and Helen.

"Pandy, don't do it! This is crazy! It's absurd! It's *incongruous*! It's . . ."

"Shut *up*, dummy!" Helen reached around and snatched the box out Pandy's hand. The two girls examined it carefully, not touching the red seal.

"This doesn't look so horrible. It's just a box. And there's no lock on it. Zeus would never trust your loser dad with evil in a box with no lock," said Hippia.

"Whatever," said Pandy. "Now give it back."

"Maybe. In a minute. We'll see," said Helen, the fake sweetness gone. Pandy realized the enormity of her mistake. These girls were never, ever going to accept her or her friends. They were just as mean as they'd always been. Nothing had changed.

"This isn't the seal of Zeus. Just looks like you melted some wax and drew a thunderbolt in it," said Helen, and she started to draw her finger over the great red seal.

"Don't, Helen!" Pandy shouted. "Don't touch it! You can't ever touch the seal."

"Why not? It's just a glob of wax! Probably had your little simp of a brother do some finger painting on it."

And she put her forefinger on top of the great mark of Zeus.

"See? No big . . ."

But she couldn't get her finger off the wax, which was now slowly starting to bubble and foam.

"Oh! Ahh . . ."

"Give me the box!" said Pandy.

"Take it!" screamed Helen, thrusting it toward Pandy.

But the box wouldn't leave Helen's hands. Hippia tried to wrench it away, and in doing so also touched the seal. Her hands stuck to the box like it was made of tar. The wax was melting and steaming away in a fine mist that splattered and burned Helen and Hippia, and they were screaming wildly. And then, in the middle of their foreheads, both girls began to grow wide, curving, black horns. Then their teeth began to go wide and flat in their mouths. Pandy had only heard tales of creatures called rhinoceroses—until now. Iole had backed up to the cupboards, but Pandy and Alcie were rooted where they stood.

"Gods, I'm sorry. I'm sorry. I'm sorry," Pandy whispered over and over, watching the girls undergo their transformation. Suddenly, with a force of will she didn't know she had, she unrooted herself and swiftly leapt forward. She grabbed the back of the box, and gave a tremendous tug. The box easily left Helen's and Hippia's hands, but the force of Pandy's pull and lack of wax on the adamantine clasp caused the lid to fly open toward Pandy.

With a start, she dropped the box, which landed only inches from Helen and Hippia.

There was a tremendous crack of thunder.

Nothing horrible came out. Nothing came out at all.

There was a long pause.

"Look at me!" screamed Hippia, her words sounding mushy over her big teeth. "I will totally get you for this, you little . . ."

Just then, the ground started to shake slightly.

"Look," whispered Iole.

A black tendril of smoke was creeping slowly out of the box. It was joined by a green tendril, and then a gray one. Brown, red, rust, yellow. One by one, an ugly rainbow of smoke was rising into the sky. The smoke started to pour out faster and faster until it was a geyser. Stumbling, Helen and Hippia got too close to the torrent and brushed against it.

Instantly, both girls began to shape-shift very quickly, changing from rhinos to large whiskered rats to spotted razorback boars to pink-and-red-striped pythons to overgrown lime green skinks and everything in between. Their skin hardened into brown leather, crystallized into scales, then became coarse gray fur. Bristle hairs the thickness of bush twigs sprouted from pointed pigs' ears as they changed from serpents to swine. Their misshapen feet became talons, morphed into hooves, then claws, and at last disappeared entirely. Finally, they turned into large black legless salamanders, gasping for breath and flopping on the stones like fishes.

The torrent of smoke continued with a roar. Then it stopped abruptly. Pandy stared at the box. She saw something like a fine silvery mist slowly start to rise. She quickly snapped the lid shut. On its own, the adamant clasp flipped back into place. The ground was shaking violently and Pandy could see the sky now streaked with lines of red, yellow, and gray, flying fast over the countryside in all different directions. Loud wails and cries were starting to erupt throughout Athens.

Pandy had no idea what she was doing when she picked up the little box. She only knew she had to get it back home. She turned, sobbing, to her friends.

"Run!" she cried. "Run, run, run!"

Alcie took off like a deer, but Iole was just staring at what used to be Helen and Hippia. Pandy grabbed her hand and pulled her along the portico. The new school buildings were crumbling around them. The marble columns at the front entrance were tottering precariously, and they barely missed being hit by pieces of the roof as it slid off. Students were fleeing in all directions. Pandy heard a loud explosion behind her and, looking back, saw a tall spurt of red ash coming from the middle of the school. So the rumor was true, the amphitheater *was* on top of a volcano!

She ran fast, past collapsing buildings and uprooted trees. Past people stumbling about, hurt and crying and confused.

Not one of the girls stopped running over the shaking ground, around flooded streams, past overturned oxcarts and tumbling boulders, until each was at home under her own pallet.

CHAPTER SIX

Back Home

"Pandora!"

Prometheus burst through the outer door and into the main room, tripping over a sea green floor pillow and knocking down two costly antique oil lamps.

"Pandora . . . get down here!"

Sybilline stood in the hall before the large looking glass, adjusting her silver girdle and giving her cheeks a last pinch, trying to make herself resemble the nymphs in the frescoes painted on the walls around her.

"Where is she, Syb?"

"She's upstairs in her room, I suppose. She ran past me a few lines on the sundial ago. Why are you yelling?" She caught sight of him in the glass. "Prometheus, what have you got on?"

"Wet straw, muck, mud . . . you name it!" Prometheus covered the floor with huge, angry strides. "I, the strongest and cleverest of the Titans! I, who held fire in the palm of my hand, who chained the Stymphalian Birds, who listened unharmed to the Sirens' song, who picked out the fiercest three-headed pup for Hades' guard dog! And now, I'm covered in . . . muck."

He slumped the only clean part of himself, his shoulder, against the wall.

"I knew something was wrong when I saw the sky darken so early. I didn't even finish the Atropos family atrium. Haven't you been listening to the runners? The whole city is in ruins!"

She gave a short laugh.

"No, Syb . . . I mean it's really in ruins. I'm not talking about the way they keep the Acropolis Museum and Theme Park for the tourists. The new Parthenon is on fire. Mount Hymettus is spewing lava. The Aegean is cresting the sea wall. I saw it all. And people have gone insane. The Menelaus twins? Those nice boys with the father who's always at war? They were in the paddock as I passed their house! They ran over and picked up a handful of this . . ."

He looked down at his toga.

". . . I don't even want to think about what it is . . . they threw a wad as big as your head right at me. And where, exactly, do you think you're going?"

Sybilline gave herself a last look.

"I'm late for work."

"You're not going to work!"

"Shh . . . keep your voice down!"

"Syb," he whispered, "I know you stopped listening to anything I have to say a long time ago . . ."

"Oh, you silly . . . ," she clucked.

"But I forbid you to go to work!"

"You *forbid?*" Sybilline turned to her husband and gently tugged on his beard. "That's very funny. I'm sure the temple office is still open."

"Fine. Just great," Prometheus said. "The city is crumbling because of your daughter and you're going to work to take dictation from the God of Heaven."

"Honey, if you don't lower your voice," said Sybilline, "he'll chain you back to that rock and let his eagle go feasting on your innards again. And what do you mean 'my daughter'? What has Pandora done?"

"You'll see! I knew it . . . I knew we shouldn't have kept it in the house. Pandora!" he called again. "She took it . . . the little thief!"

Sybilline glanced out at the garden sundial.

"Yes, well, whatever it is . . . deal with it as you think best."

"Oh, I'm going to . . . just you watch."

But his wife was already out the door.

"Pandora!" he yelled, striding over to the bottom of the stairway. "Pan—"

"What?"

Pandy stood just above the curve of the stairs, next to

the altar of Athena, one arm wrapped tightly around her training girdle, the other hand fiddling with a piece of sacrificial goat.

Prometheus cleared his throat. He started to pace the length of the room.

"Hi there."

"Hi, Dad."

"How ya doin'?"

" 'kay."

"How's things?"

"Fine."

"How's school?"

"Good."

"Anything new happen today?"

"Um . . . like what?"

"Oh, I don't know," Prometheus said. "Like maybe you got your algebra test back? Maybe you saw that boy you really like? Maybe you stole the box from under my bed and released the greatest evils ever created into the world? Anything like *that* happen today?"

"Oh."

"Yeah, oh! Where is it?"

"It's next to my diary."

He shot past her on the stairs.

"Come on, missy."

She followed him to her room.

"Get it, please."

Pandy got the box from the wooden shelf where she'd hidden it.

"Come on," said her father, and she followed him into her parents' room. Prometheus pulled out Sybilline's jewel box from under the pallet. Then he grabbed two small clay jars from a high shelf.

"Now *this* one," he said, thrusting the jewel box under her nose. "*This* is the box you knew you could take to school! This is the *show and tell* box! You can play with anything in *here!*

"And you know where I keep my liver!" he went on, waving one of the small clay jars.

"Or here . . . ," he said, holding up the other jar. "Here's a little bit of the eternal flame. Not many kids have this lying around the house."

Prometheus was starting to turn purple, the veins in his forehead looked ready to burst.

He put Sybilline's jewel box back and brought out the carved metal and onyx case. "But *this* was off limits! No touching!" He shook the case gently. "Hmm . . . sounds empty! Why is that, only ill-begotten daughter of Prometheus? Is it because you stole the wooden box that was in here?"

"Dad . . ."

"Yes?"

"Dad . . . I couldn't bring your liver to school. Not again. You can't even tell what it is anymore."

"What about the fire?"

"Fire's no big deal now."

"But fire is a family friend, Pandora! It's very much an enduring presence," he said. "You could have blown on some ashes, for Hades' sake! You could have heated the whole school!"

"You made me promise not to show that to anyone!"

"I ALSO MADE YOU PROMISE NOT TO TOUCH THE BOX!"

"Oh . . . yeah."

"What about your mother's Zeus presents?" Prometheus said.

"Geez, Dad, look around . . . all the kids' moms have stuff from Zeus!"

"So all that business about corn cakes and talking about Demeter . . . that was just a bunch of . . . well, it sure was, wasn't it? You must really take your father for a fool, Pandora. Well, I guess you showed us all, didn't you?"

Pandora felt more miserable than she could ever remember. She held the wooden box out to him.

"Dad, I never, ever meant for it to be opened, I swear! I just told everyone what it was and that no one could ever open it 'cause if they did all of the evil things inside would get out and mankind would be miserable forever."

"And?"

"And then I started home to put it back under your pallet."

Prometheus clenched his jaw.

"Well, when . . . did . . . you . . . open . . . it?"

"It was later . . . Helen-and-Hippia-came-up-to-me-and-told-me-that-I-could-come-to-a-pre-Bacchanalia-party-and-that-Alcie-and-Iole-could-come-too-but-only-if-they-could-see-the-box. I *so* didn't think it would matter if they just looked at it. But before I knew it, it was too late."

"As if a liver-eating eagle wasn't enough in my life-time," Prometheus said, taking the wooden box. "Do you have any idea exactly what was in here?"

Just then, there was the sound of another volcanic eruption from the direction of the middle school.

"Well, I kinda do now."

"Kinda, Pandora? Kinda? Well, let me tell you *exactly* what was in this box. Ares . . . God of War? He put in Rage. The kind of rage that makes people want to tear each other to shreds for no reason at all. Apollo and Artemis put in Vanity. Average citizens will sit at their looking glasses for days on end, oohing and aahing over themselves until they starve. Athena put in Greed, but not simply the 'Oh, I'd like to have a few more drachmas in my pocket' kind. No. It's the type of greed that makes a son kill his parents for the last crust of flatbread.

"There was only one beautiful thing that was kept in this box, and that was Hope. Why? Because we just didn't need Hope if there was nothing to make us despair. Maybe I should have told you exactly how bad it would be if you disobeyed me, but I thought that you were old enough that my word alone was all you needed. I guess I was wrong."

"Oh, Dad," she started to really sob. "I'm so sorry."

"Uh-huh." Prometheus was tired. He put everything away but the wooden box. "Okay . . . no diary for an entire season. And you're going to sleep on the floor. No staying late after sacrifices to talk with any youths . . ."

At that moment, Sybilline blew sideways into the sleeping room; her girdle askew, a lump growing on the side of her forehead.

"I couldn't get to the temple! There's rioting in the streets. People are driving their chariots on the wrong side of the roads. Lava is covering everything, centaurs are looting the marketplace, and my manicure is ruined! I'm afraid Zeus will think I quit without two weeks' notice! What will happen to my severance package . . . and my insurance benefits? Oh no"—she began to tear at her golden hair—"you remember what he did to me three months ago . . . when I didn't show up on time for my job interview . . ."

Suddenly, a bolt of lightning shot out of the ceiling,

and Sybilline was reduced to a cloud of ashes, floating gently down to cover two charred sandals and a girdle.

Prometheus stood over what used to be his wife.

"Happy, Pandora? Look what you made Zeus do to your mother—again!"

Once before, when she'd been scheduled to meet Zeus for her initial job interview, Sybilline had stayed too long at Calypso's Clay Pot Beauty Emporium. Zeus was so enraged at her obvious lack of interest that he vaporized Sybilline with a thunderbolt as she was having her toenails painted. It was only after much begging by Prometheus to Athena that Zeus restored her.

"Sabina!" Prometheus called downstairs. "I need an urn, please! And bring a broom."

"Get them yourself, you good-for-nothing, cloven-hoofed goat!" came the answer.

"Sabina, now, please!" he roared. "Do you see now, Pandora? Do you see what happens when the world is infected with pettiness, contempt, and insolence? Sabina has been with us for years, and now listen to her. That's the first sign of disrespect."

The ancient woman shuffled into the room holding a broom and an urn.

"Here you go, but don't expect . . ."

She shrieked, seeing the sandals and silver girdle lying under a pile of ashes.

"Oh, Gods, not again!"

"Sabina, will you please clean up my wife?"

As Sabina started to sweep, Prometheus knelt and whispered to the pile, "Honey, I don't know if you can hear me, but I'll try to get you restored again as soon as the lava cools."

He turned to Pandy.

"*And* . . . you're grounded for the next three moons. *And* I want you to write an apology to your school principal, *and* . . . wait a minute! What's this?"

From the wooden box, still gripped in his hand, a faint whooshing sound could be heard. He shook the box gently.

"Great Aphrodite . . . something's still in here! Pandora, when you opened the box . . . tell me exactly what you saw!"

"Um, after all the black and green and red things flew away, there was something kinda misty and silvery trying to get out. So I closed the lid fast!"

"Misty and silvery?" he said. "And . . . and . . . you closed the lid? Well, of course you did. How would you know, right? Pandora, you closed the lid on Hope. Hope is still trapped inside."

"Is that good? No. No, that's bad. Gods, I can't do anything right."

"Pandora!" He spoke sharply, as Sabina handed him

the urn with his wife. "Stop it this instant! This isn't about you anymore. Look at the city! Think of the people!"

He began to pace.

"I have to . . . to . . . think. Should I . . . open it? No . . . there might be something else besides Hope . . . another evil. Better not take a . . . a . . . chance. I have to think!"

He stopped abruptly and looked at his daughter.

"Pandora!" he said. "Pandora, on top of everything else, you've left the world without Hope!"

CHAPTER SEVEN

Apology

Dear Principal Diogenes,

I am very sorry I released evil into the world yesterday during the school project. My dad has grounded me for three moons, and I'll miss the Spring Bacchanalia. But I deserve it.

My mother probably won't be at my parent/master conference next week because Zeus turned her into a pile of ashes (again).

Please don't expel me.

If I had known any of this would happen, I would have brought my dad's liver (again).

Sincerely,
Pandora,
daughter of Prometheus of Athens
Maiden, Master Epeus's class

P.S. Helen of Sparta and Hippia of Thornax are in the portico. If you find two things that look like black lizards, that's them.

CHAPTER EIGHT

A Visit

There was a violent jolt, a blinding flash, and the walls of her room began to glow white hot. Dido, who had been lying at her feet, yelped and hid under her pallet. Another jolt shook the house. She staggered out into the hallway. Prometheus, Xander in his arms, was just emerging from his room. Everything was glowing like the inside of a furnace. As quickly as it began, the shaking stopped and the glowing walls returned to normal. But there was a brilliant light shining up the stairwell from the main room below.

Sabina was just reaching the top of the stairs, panting hard.

"You've . . . you've got company!"

Prometheus headed down the stairs, with Pandy and Sabina close behind.

Descending into the bright light, Prometheus had to shield his eyes. He stopped suddenly at the bottom of the stairs, unable to see. Pandy and Sabina crashed into him from behind like a chariot wreck.

"Prometheus!"

They all heard a voice coming through the light, high pitched yet booming.

"Prometheus, you are summoned!"

Prometheus stood still a moment.

"Hermes?" he finally said.

"It is I."

"Well, cut the light already!" Prometheus said, handing Xander to Sabina.

At once the light disappeared, and standing in the middle of the room was the most beautiful being Pandy had ever seen. He was dressed in a short, shimmering silver toga and there were golden wings on his sandals. And he was so tall that the fluttering wings on his golden helmet brushed against the bottom of the ceiling. He held an odd twisted gold wand in his huge hand.

Hermes, Messenger of the Gods, the swiftest, shrewdest, and most cunning of all the Olympians, faced the family of Prometheus, arms folded and a tremendous scowl on his face.

Neither the god nor Prometheus spoke for a moment, then Hermes broke into a huge grin and the two grabbed each other in a great hug.

"Good to see you, Prometheus!" he said.

"And you, my friend."

"Hey, sorry about the light," Hermes said. "Standard procedure. Zeus wants everyone to be terribly afraid when I appear, whether it's good news or bad; but that kind of thinking is *so* Bronze Age, right? If I bring good news, I only have to shine a little. But if it's a message of punishment and doom, I have to really turn on the brights. Blinding flashes, heart-stopping fear, that sort of thing."

"Well, I guess I'm in big trouble then, huh?" said Prometheus.

"Not you so much as the girl. It's really your daughter he wants to see. Is this her?" asked Hermes, pointing to Pandy.

"Yes. Pandora," he said, pulling Pandy toward the god. "This is Hermes, Zeus's messenger, Master Thief, holder of the Caduceus . . ."

The thing in his hand, thought Pandy.

". . . professional lyre maker and protector of traders and merchants."

"Oh, please! Stop already, you're making me blush!"

Hermes gave Prometheus a giant pat on the back that almost sent him flying across the room. He wasn't acting the way Pandora had expected. He wasn't blustery or pompous. He was kinda fun, in a wacky sort of way.

"Hi, Pandora," he said, smiling. He leaned casually

against the wall, which immediately started to separate from the rest of the house.

"Um . . . hi."

"Listen," Hermes went on, "forget all that stuff you just heard. I'm basically an errand boy. You know your dad and I go way, way back. Hey, let's have a look at you. Wow, Pandora! Are you gonna look like your mom when you get older. Am I right, Prometheus? Well, that is if Zeus lets you live. Oh, forget I said that! Okay . . . it's time we got going!"

"Who's 'we,' my friend?" said Prometheus, panic creeping into his voice. "She's not going. The box was mine to protect—my responsibility! Leave her here, Hermes."

"No can do, Pro. I've got my orders." He snapped his fingers and a small sheepskin scroll appeared in midair, unrolled itself flat, and declaimed in a squeaky voice: *"The House of Prometheus of Athens is hereby summoned to appear for judgment before the Sky-Lord and Cloud-Gatherer, Zeus. And, yes, Prometheus . . . that means everybody."*

At the bottom of the scroll was the great red wax seal of Zeus.

"Hermes, I'm begging you . . . ," Prometheus started.

"Look"—Hermes dropped his voice to a whisper—"you think I'm enjoying this? One second of it? I'm not, okay? This is serious, my friend. I'm trying my best to be jolly because I don't want to scare the girl any more than necessary. Now, you can make this easy or hard, your choice."

Too confused to panic, Pandy felt as if she were somewhere high above her body looking down on an exciting scene. But she couldn't comprehend that she was actually a part of it.

Prometheus hung his face in his hands.

"We'll go. We'll all go."

"Of course you will! Like you really had a choice, am I right?" Hermes said, the joviality back in his voice. "Now, what size sandal do you take, Pandora?"

"Huh?"

Nice. Oh, she was really making a good impression, she thought.

"What size are your sandals?" Hermes asked again, repeating the words more slowly this time.

"Oh . . . size six."

"Very good." Hermes snapped his fingers again and, in a flash of gold sparks, a large wooden shoe rack appeared in the middle of the room. On it were dozens of pairs of men's and women's sandals. Each pair was different; some encrusted with jewels, some lined with exotic furs, a few even had heels.

"There we go," said Hermes, handing her a pair of bright pink leather sandals with tiny diamonds on the laces and two silver wings on each side. "These should fit. And the color goes great with your hair. But don't go getting any ideas, cutie-pie . . . these aren't for buyin', they're for flyin'. I need these back if . . . I mean *when* we return from Olympus."

"Olympus?" said Pandy.

"Yep," said Hermes. "We're all gonna take a little trip."

He handed Prometheus a pair of sandals lined in fox fur with bronze wings. Sabina tied tiny rabbit-trimmed and gold-winged sandals on Xander. Hermes handed her a pair with lead wings that looked like they were made from a large snake.

"Could I see something in a mink maybe, with . . . ?" Sabina said.

"Take what you get! Just think of it as fate . . . ," Hermes said.

"Yes, yes, of course . . . thanks," she said, wrinkling her nose behind his back. "Oh, very clever . . . fate! Very funny," she mumbled.

"Are we all strapped in? Ready? Wait . . . Prometheus, where's your wife?" said Hermes.

"Oh Gods, she's still upstairs in her urn!"

"Never mind. I'll pick her up on the way," said Hermes.

He waved his Caduceus and Pandy felt a small vibration in her feet. She looked down to see the small silver wings flapping furiously. The next instant she felt herself propelled upward through the ceiling, which parted for her like it was made of foam. Tiny bits of clay brushed against her skin and, as she was drawn up through the floor of her sleeping room, she could feel the slight scratch of the floor tapestries. She saw Dido's white face for only a moment as she whizzed on up toward the roof of the house. She felt the coolness of the tiles as they dematerialized to let her pass. A second later she was out into the crisp night air. It was still light enough to see the devastation that had befallen Athens in only a few hours. The whole city looked as if it were on fire. Buildings had collapsed in on themselves. There was a huge break in the sea wall and the Aegean was flooding nearby farmland, ruining it for centuries to come. Mobs of people were in the streets with nowhere to go, nowhere to turn.

A few moments later she saw something black circling her head for just a second. She felt a soft touch, like a hand cupping her face gently, then a whisper in her ear, "Now, Pandora," before the black shape disappeared. She felt herself falling into a deep sleep, almost like a faint, but before she completely lost consciousness, she saw her father fighting to stand upright in his sandals a short distance away, his hand holding tight to Xander's arm. She saw Sabina passed out cold, her snakeskin sandals struggling to keep pace with the others. She watched as Hermes streaked past all of them like a comet, her mother's urn held close to his side. And she saw the lights of her house, then Athens, then the world get smaller and smaller as she passed into darkness.

CHAPTER NINE
Olympus

In the instant before her eyes opened, Pandy thought that everything she had seen and done only moments (hours? days?) before had all been a dream. She stretched out, expecting the feel of well-worn cotton pallet sheets.

Instead, her limbs brushed against . . . what? What was she lying on? She opened her eyes and saw nothing but white, not bright but soft and gentle: white walls, white sky outside the paneless windows, and a big puffy white bed. Her whole body was surrounded by a billowy, bulbous substance that she could poke through with her fingers yet, somehow, supported her weight. It was damp to the touch, but her toga was still dry.

"Clouds!" she said. "I'm lying on clouds."

"Ah, you're awake," said a tender chorus of voices.

Pandy was startled into silence.

"Hello?" she whispered at length.

"Hello!"

"Who are you?" asked Pandy, now frightened.

"We are daughters of daughters of daughters of Zeus."

Little pink mouths and tiny pairs of eyes in vibrant blues, greens, and grays began to appear, hovering in midair; all staring at her.

"You have been summoned. Arise!" said the mouths in unison.

With that, the cloud bed evaporated instantly and Pandy saw below her a steep expanse of a jagged, rocky mountaintop. She was going to fall to her death! But before she could panic, the vision was replaced by a white marble floor and she found herself standing upright and very wide-awake.

A door in the room swung outward and Pandy felt unseen hands gently push her through the opening and down a long, impossibly high, white marble hallway. The air was perfumed with lavender and honeysuckle. Oil lamps in the shape of great eagles hung from the ceiling on long gold chains, their flames burning brightly even though the very walls seemed to be made of light itself. What really captivated her, though, were the fountains. At various intervals, in the middle of a shallow pool that ran the length of the hallway, were large fountains in the forms of the original Titans, the rulers of the earth and sky before their war with Zeus and the other great gods of Olympus.

There was Cronus, father of Zeus, wrestling in vain with his son. Zeus's mother, Rhea, was shown weeping, the water in the fountain flowing from her eyes. Another Titan, Oceanus, ruler of the rivers and seas before Poseidon, was depicted being subdued by his own waves. One of the most beautiful fountains was of the Titan Mnemosyne, whose name meant Memory, holding a large hourglass as if perhaps she knew the days of the Titans were at an end.

Pandy gazed at these and others as the hands guided her toward two large golden doors, which swung inward to reveal a dim amber light. Pandy was just about to walk through when she looked up at the face of the last fountain.

She gasped and stopped in her tracks.

Was it? No . . . it couldn't be, she thought. But it was true.

It was her father.

Prometheus, in full battle armor, his muscles taut and a long sword raised high above his head in victory.

"Huh?" she said aloud.

The invisible hands pushed harder now and Pandy almost stumbled as she passed through the golden doors.

She entered a hall the size of the amphitheater back at the Athena Maiden Middle School. The hands were steering her toward the center, where Pandy could just make out an enormous golden table, over which hung a single oil lamp as big around as an eagle's nest . . . if it were a really huge eagle. As she got closer, weaving her way through gigantic columns, she saw that the table wasn't quite circular; it was a teardrop.

Standing in front of the large, fat end, Sabina held a sleeping Xander in her arms alongside her father, who clutched the urn containing her mother.

Pandy stepped into line with the others and looked first at her father . . . the Titan. He was staring, grim faced, straight ahead. But when he felt his daughter next to him, he looked down at her and smiled.

"Hi, honey," he said.

Pandy started to cry. She was more confused than scared, but she didn't want to look in front of her; she desperately didn't want to see who or what was at the head of the table.

"Oh, Daddy . . ."

"Don't cry, sweetheart. We'll be fine," he said, but he didn't sound convincing. "Look up now."

Pandy turned her head.

At a distance behind the teardrop table were hundreds of large robed figures, men and women, some holding strange objects, some wearing garlands, a few had the lower bodies of goats and horses, many looked to be very wet. She squinted: these must be all the immortals of Greece, she thought. Pandy only recognized a few. There was Aeolus, King of the Winds, his blue-tipped hair flying wildly about his head and the skin on his face pulled back as if he were standing in the middle of a violent storm. She saw Pan, son of Hermes, half-man, half-goat, picking a stone out of one of his hooves. Helios, whose palace housed the sun that Apollo's chariot drove across the heavens, seemed to have the sun inside of him: his eyes, mouth, and ears radiated light. There, in the corner, was Iris, the Goddess of the Rainbow, her skin streaked in broad bands of every color.

All of the lesser gods must be here too, she thought, and the river and wood nymphs, satyrs, and the half-man, half-horse centaurs. Then she summoned up her courage and looked around the enormous table.

The great gods of Olympus were staring straight at her.

Closest to Pandy, but still a good distance away, sat Demeter, Goddess of Corn, the Harvest, and the Seasons. Her hair was magnificent—long strands of greenish tendrils with hundreds of little spring flowers. But as Pandy watched, the tendrils turned into the parched, cracked wheat grass of summer and then immediately changed into dry twigs sprouting dying autumn leaves in fiery colors, until at last her head was covered with icicles. Then, before Pandy's eyes, the whole cycle started again.

Hephaestus, God of the Forge and Fire, sat in his chair, grimy and covered with soot, cleaning his teeth with a bronze toothpick. He was a brilliant metalworker and the maker of Zeus's thunderbolts, with the muscles of his upper body rivaling those of Hercules in their size and strength. But his lower body was small, scarcely larger than a baby's, and hideously misshapen.

Ares, God of War and son of Zeus, was seated at the table in full battle dress; his breastplate and arm guards splattered with layers of dried black blood. Gross! Pandy thought. Only his yellow eyes were visible between the slits in his helmet, but every few moments hot steam shot out from the breathing hole. He cracked his knuckles occasionally, a huge fierce-looking dog at his side.

Another son of Zeus, Apollo, God of the Sun and Music and Healing, sat restringing his golden lyre, plucking the strings gently every so often. Even in those single notes, Pandy had never heard music as beautiful. If Zeus let her live, she would tell Iole that she actually saw the god who gave Iole back her life.

Closest to the head of the table sat Zeus's brother Poseidon, Lord of the all the Waters, blowing his nose into a damp cloth, desperately fighting his allergy to shellfish. Pandy saw his lower body was that of a shiny green fish and his chair was partially submerged in a large tank of water. Occasionally his tail would flip, sending droplets of water flying (and sizzling when they hit Ares' armor).

Across the table was Aphrodite, the beautiful and beguiling. The Goddess of Love was smiling sweetly, staring at her lover, Ares, and steadfastly avoiding the looks from her husband, Hephaestus. Pandy thought that all the light in the entire hall must have been coming from her smile. Two doves perched on her shoulders, cooing as she occasionally reached out for her son Eros, the little Love-God (and whose name also meant romantic love), as he ran about the great hall shooting arrows at everyone.

Zeus's son Dionysus, God of Wine, snored gently, his head slumped slightly forward, the circlet of grapes and vines he wore having fallen over one ear.

At his right was Artemis, Goddess of the Moon and the gods' official huntress. She was also the giver of Pandy's wolfskin diary. She was replacing the silver string on her great bow without even looking at her hands; her sad eyes focused solely on Pandy.

Athena, the Goddess of Wisdom, was having a quiet conversation with the owl perched on her wrist. Athena, like the others, was also looking directly at Pandy, but there was something kind in her leaf green eyes. Pandy realized that the simple statue in its niche back home didn't come close to her true magnificence.

And then Pandy saw Zeus's wife, Hera, in her magnificent blue robes, a crown of peacock feathers on her head. She sat very still, but her thin mouth was clenching and unclenching every few seconds. The poets called Hera "chief among the immortals in beauty." She was lovely indeed, but looking at Aphrodite and Athena, Pandy thought the poets didn't know what they were talking about.

Hermes stood a little to the right of a majestic golden throne that occupied a space where the table came to a point, a much more serious look on his face now than she'd seen before.

The only one missing is Hades, Dark Lord of the Underworld, thought Pandy, I wonder where . . .

Then, as if given a signal, all eyes turned their gaze from the foursome at the end of the table to the one who sat on the golden throne.

Zeus, the Supreme Ruler, Lord of the Sky, whose power was greater than all other gods combined, sat slightly above the others. He was older, but handsome. His silver hair and beard cascaded over his gleaming white robes. The muscles of his upper body were so big, Pandy couldn't have stretched both of her arms around one of his. And he was staring down, through ice blue eyes, from underneath glowering silver eyebrows, at her.

Pandy felt the breath go out of her body. She wanted to faint; she wanted to simply go to sleep right then and there and never, ever wake up. She wanted to die. Or better, she wanted to pass out and wake up in a blanket of clouds again and just stay there forever.

"You wish to flee, Pandora? To run? Are those the thoughts in your tiny mind?" said Zeus. "You could not now—nor ever—escape me." His voice sounded like it should have hurt her ears, yet it didn't. He must be softening it somehow, she thought, otherwise we'd all be deaf. But it also sounded old and a little . . . a little . . . what was it? Pandy thought. Tired, she realized, he's tired.

"I would follow you, daughter of Prometheus. I would follow you down to the depths of your dreams to tell you what I have to say. I would hunt you into the flames of Tartarus and bring you back for the punishment you deserve. You have doomed mankind, *your* kind, to age upon age of sorrow. And why did you do this? So you would be popular with fools? So you would be accepted among those not fit to wash your feet? So you could feel special, not knowing that feeling comes from doing what is right for all, not merely what is right for *you*. And you dare to hope you can escape me in death? After what you have done, your negligence, your recklessness, your selfishness, your lack of caring for your fellow man, and your obvious contempt for my will and my wisdom and that of all the gods; DO YOU THINK DEATH WOULD HINDER ME AT ALL?"

Prometheus put an arm around Pandy.

"Sky-Lord, you frighten my daughter."

"Silence, Titan!" Zeus trained his eyes on Prometheus. "Or your tongue will curl in your mouth and remain that way! She should be frightened. Have you never told her our happy little tale, Prometheus? Does she not know what I am capable of?"

Zeus glared at Sabina. "And you," he said. "Still happy with your decision to leave Olympus? Perhaps you should have stayed here, toiling away at my drainage counters, hmm?"

Sabina clutched the sleeping Xander tightly in her arms and, standing as straight as she could, met the eyes of the Cloud-Gatherer with a steady if slightly nearsighted gaze.

"I foresaw you getting too big for your toga . . . and look at you!" she said clearly.

Zeus chuckled. Then he looked back at Pandora.

"If it were up to me—and it is—I would have the House of Prometheus boiling in oil for the first ten thousand years of eternity, then I would have you all cleaning the sewage pits in the underworld for a bit, then some dish washing in the dining hall in the Elysian Fields, then you'd spend some time in the fire pits of Tartarus . . . and then things would really get bad."

Pandy clung to her father's waist and tried to hide her face in his toga.

"Look at me, little one!" roared Zeus. "It just so happens that my extremely generous nature has been prevailed upon. The Queen of Heaven has taken pity on you, child, even though, with some of the evils you released into the universe, her temples have been most desecrated and her name most taken in vain. You will offer her your gratitude now."

Pandy looked at the great Hera with surprise. From what she'd been told of Hera's disposition ever since she could listen to the storytellers, Hera had taken pity on no one . . . ever.

"Thank you, mighty Hera." Pandy's voice was lost in the echo of the hall. Prometheus gave her shoulders a tiny squeeze.

"Louder! My wife did not hear you!" said Zeus.

"Thank you, mighty and wonderful goddess!" she said, a little too loudly this time. Pandy thought she saw Hermes laugh slightly to himself.

Hera smiled graciously in Pandy's direction and nodded her perfectly coiffed head. But Hera did not really look at her and Pandy noticed that, ever so slightly, the other gods at the table shifted their eyes to one another briefly.

"I have an offer for you, Pandora," said Zeus. "You and your family will not be tortured through infinite eternity if, and only if, you accept it."

Pandy had absolutely no idea what was coming but

she was sure it wasn't going to be something like sleeping on the floor for a moon or writing a letter to her principal.

"Each of the plagues you foolishly released has found a home somewhere on earth. There are seven great evils . . . and assorted lesser ones. You alone of your family will find each of them at the purest source and return them to the box. Where is the box, Hermes?"

"My lord, inside the bronze case."

"Ah yes, the case," said Zeus, looking at Prometheus. "Well, a lot of good *that* did."

His eyes shifted back to Pandy.

"Let no one in your family come to your aid. You have one half-cycle of the seasons, six phases of the moon, in which to accomplish this, and if you succeed, which is most highly doubtful, you and your family will be allowed your natural lives. If you do not accept or if you fail, which, considering the nature of your crime, I must say I'm rather looking forward to, well . . . I've already mentioned a few of the delights I have in store for you. I see no need to ruin all the surprises. Apollo will fly his sun chariot in the sky once and that is all the time you will have to prepare for your departure. What is your answer?"

Pandy was so shocked by what she'd just heard that, at first, she made no sound.

"I . . . I . . . have to find them?" she stammered.

"What is your answer?" Zeus boomed.

"My lord," Prometheus said, trying to strike a balance between showing the proper respect, maintaining his dignity, and defending his daughter, "the box was in my keeping. The offense is mine. She is only a silly, willful girl. She is my flesh and therefore I love her, but she is difficult and childish. Let this undertaking fall to me."

Pandy looked up at her father and felt like a knife had sliced into her stomach. Zeus had called her many things: *reckless, selfish,* and *contemptuous*. But nothing he'd said had hit her the way the words *silly, difficult,* and *childish* had coming out of her father's mouth. She had most assuredly disappointed him and quite probably condemned him. And the horrible reality struck her like another physical blow: it was all true. All because of her curiosity. This was, without question, the worst moment of her life. Then, it was as if an invisible rope latched on to the words in her head and dragged them, kicking and screaming, out of her mouth.

"I'll do it," she said, very quietly.

"What was that, Pandora?" Hera said quickly.

Pandora tried to stand a little straighter. She had no idea what she was saying yes to, she only knew the fault was all hers and she was going to try to make it right.

"I said I'll do it . . . great Hera. I'll get them back. All of them. At least I'll try."

CHAPTER TEN
Many Questions

Pandy knew that her life, if she had one, was never going to be the same.

She was aware that her father's legs were trembling slightly. She squeezed his hand.

"Very good. It will be interesting to watch your progress, or not," said Zeus. "And now, fare—"

"Father," Hermes spoke up.

"—well. What? What do you require?"

Hermes leaned low toward Zeus and turned his face away from the far end of the table. Pandy heard soft mumbling between the two gods, then Zeus suddenly banged his right hand on the arm of his golden throne and Pandy watched his silver eyebrows rise into his hair.

"What? You mean it's still in the box?" he growled. "Well, she's an inept little thing, isn't she?"

Zeus waved Hermes away.

"I have just been informed, Pandora," he said, "that Hope did not escape with the great sorrows, but is still imprisoned . . ."

He paused, gazing on some point deep in the recesses of the great hall, silent for a long time. Pandy thought his shoulders sagged just a little before he looked at her again.

"And that is where it shall stay. You have accepted this task and you shall succeed or fail while watching mankind labor under the misery you created. Witness the full measure of the world's despair, beset by evil and bereft of Hope. May you learn from this punishment. And now . . ."

"Father!" Hermes said quickly.

". . . farewe— *What*?"

"Should we not give her the map?"

"Ah, yes . . . I do need to give you a fighting chance, I suppose," said Zeus. "For just such a contingency that an accident should occur—for instance, a ridiculous little girl would somehow open the box—a map was created to locate each sorrow and return it back to the box. Use it properly, and it will direct you to the pure source of each great plague. Hera, dearest, the map."

Hera rose and walked portentously toward Pandy, raising her right hand above her head, twirling it gracefully two times. A thin, yellowed sheepskin bag appeared out of the air. The pouch was tied with a golden string and sealed with a small drop of blue wax, stamped with the figure of Hera's peacock.

"There you are, my child. This will tell you all you need to know to succeed." She lowered her head slightly and whispered to Pandy, "Which, if I may say, I have *every* confidence that you will do!"

Pandy felt a twinge of distrust shoot through her like the pains in her legs when she was much smaller and her bones were growing faster that her muscles. Something was very wrong, but she wasn't sure just what exactly.

She did have dozens of questions, however. What did Zeus mean, use the map properly? How did she capture the plagues? What did they look like? How would she get from one place to another? She looked around the table. The other gods were looking at her, some with curiosity, some with pity. But Athena and Artemis actually smiled at her and suddenly she felt better than she had in days.

"And now, farewell!" said Zeus. "Hermes, away!"

"Zeus," said Prometheus, holding out the jar containing Sybilline, "I beg of you to restore my wife! Your mighty thunderbolt took her and I ask that you reverse—"

"Your wife? My thunderbolt?" sputtered Zeus, quickly looking at Hera. The other gods hung their heads trying to hide the faintest hints of smiles. Hera cocked a single eyebrow at her husband.

"I have no idea. I don't recall this . . . incident . . . that you speak of. You are mad in your grief to ask such things of me." Zeus paused. "But I am nothing if not charitable. Leave the urn with me and I shall think upon your request. Now, for the last time, go! Your daughter's time to prepare is dwindling fast."

Her father gently placed the urn on the great round table.

As unseen hands began pushing at Pandy again, driving her back toward the fountains, Pandora ran to catch up with her father.

"Dad! Hey, Dad . . . is that you? Dad?" She pointed up into the marble face. "Dad!"

"Not now, Pandora," he said sharply.

She went silent and fell back, only to be almost lifted off her feet by an invisible wall of poking, prodding fingers. They were guided to the left at the far end of the long hallway onto a narrow, open terrace with no railing high above the mist-shrouded peaks of Mount Olympus. Hermes was waiting for them.

"Right, then. Wasn't so bad, was it?"

"Hermes, please," said Prometheus.

"Oh, come on! You all get to live, for the time being. You got a little trip to the home of the gods and you *know* most people will never check that off their to-do lists. She"—he nodded to Pandy—"gets to go scurrying off on an adventure. Maybe you don't get your wife back, but maybe you *do,* who knows? Hey . . . good times!"

Pandy felt something soft and stringy around her feet and ankles. She looked down to see the winged pink leather sandals lacing their way up her calves.

"Pandora," said her father, "give me the map for safekeeping on the way down."

"Okay, Dad," she said, handing him the faded sheepskin bag.

They were joined on the terrace suddenly by a tall, hooded figure.

"Ah, Morpheus! Thanks for coming. Prometheus, you remember Morpheus, right? God of Dreams? Listen," Hermes whispered, but Pandy still heard it; in fact, Pandy heard everything these gods whispered. "It's just for the kids and the old woman . . . I know you can handle the ride down, but I'm iffy about them. Go ahead, Morpheus . . ."

The dark figure lifted back the hood of his cloak. Pandy saw a beautiful man with black skin, shiny black hair, and black eyes. She felt the wings of her sandals pulling her close to the edge of the terrace. Looking down for a moment, she saw only the crags of the mountain, like horrible teeth, and an endless white sky. Then Morpheus cupped a sleek black hand under her chin and turned her face toward his. He looked into her eyes and smiled the most exquisite smile she could have imagined. Instantly, sleepiness was tugging all other thoughts from her mind as the world began to fade from view. She was falling into a deep slumber and falling over the edge of the terrace at the same moment. But this time, before she went out completely, she felt Hermes flying close by and she knew she was completely safe. Then she heard him softly in her ear, "Sweet dreams."

CHAPTER ELEVEN
Good-Bye

Pandy awoke still high above the earth, but for some reason she remained unafraid. Sabina, still asleep, tottered precariously in the air, her sandals' lead wings beating frantically to keep the old woman upright. Her father, wide-awake, was flying close by with Xander in his arms, chatting with Hermes. The sun was just coming up over the hills of Athens, which she thought very strange since it had been bright daylight when they fell off the terrace. It must take hours to get up and down that mountain, she thought. Then she realized that she wasn't cold in the least, nor was there any wind, even though they were flying through the air at a tremendous speed.

Below her, she started to make out the larger buildings in the city: the Acropolis, the Parthenon, and the huge marketplace. There was the Athena Maiden Middle School. And she saw the extent of the destruction:

smoldering fires, giant rocks left in the wake of flooded rivers, trash in the streets, and cooling rivulets of lava. She started to tear up again, knowing that she was the cause. They flew low over her neighborhood, finally dropping like a stone over her home. She had several moments of extreme terror when she saw the roof of her house coming up at her fast and she started to scream, thinking she was going to be smashed like wheat berries on a grinding stone.

"Close your eyes, Pandora," came her father's voice.

She didn't have a chance to look over at him before she started descending through the roof. This time, it was simply as if she were falling into an image of her house made entirely of colored air. She closed her eyes quickly and the next moment she was coming down slowly and gently onto the floor of the family living space, standing perfectly straight and alert. Her father and Xander landed next, and then Sabina, still asleep, toppled directly onto one of the giant floor pillows and curled up like a puppy.

Landing across the room, Hermes snapped his fingers and the sandal rack appeared as before.

"Thank you very much and I hope you enjoyed your flight! Now if you'll just return your footwear to me."

Prometheus was untying Xander's fur sandals when suddenly the little boy let out a terrible wail.

"Prometheus, my friend, get your children something

to eat. It's been almost three weeks, for Olympus' sake! Here, let me . . ." Hermes waved his Caduceus and everyone's sandals began to unlace by themselves and fly to the shoe rack. Except for Pandy's, and she didn't notice because she was trying to comprehend what Hermes had just said.

They had been gone for almost three weeks?

She looked around. The family living space was just as it had always been, but then she looked closer at the food cupboards. Food was scattered all over the drainage counter and on the floor; flies hovered in the air above, dive-bombing choice morsels. Jars were spilled and their contents had dripped or fallen or coagulated everywhere. Flatbread crumbs, olive oil, and dried fruit had been tracked from tiles around the drainage counter into the living space. It wasn't as if any of the food had actually been stolen, though; more like it had been eaten through.

Dido!

He'd been without food in his bowl for almost three weeks, if Hermes was to be believed, and even if it weren't true, Dido was probably terribly worried. She'd tell him everything through her diary later.

She started to run upstairs to find him, but Hermes, with the tip of his finger, held her in place. As her father rummaged through the food cupboards, Hermes knelt before her.

"Your sandals I will remove myself," he said, looking her square in the eye.

"My dog . . . ," she gulped.

"No, you don't have to find your dog right now, Pandora. Right now, you have to listen to me."

Pandy calmed down almost involuntarily.

"You know, Pandora, some of us on Olympus were not born old and crotchety," he said, looking at her feet and almost smiling, but not quite. "Let's see. Apollo . . . and Dionysus, certainly . . . and Artemis . . . Aphrodite's seen a few things, I think . . . well, some of us do remember what it was like to be young. And foolish. Okay, let's strike that and just say stupid. A little petty thievery, a few unrequited loves, people mistakenly transformed into animals or trees or hideous monsters. Things we're not *proud* of, all right? Nothing like what you did, believe you me. But there are a few of us who have a little more understanding of *why* you did what you did. There are those who will be watching you, Pandora. A gust of wind when you least expect it. A drop of rain from a sunny sky. Maybe a pebble hits you square in the forehead to get your attention. We'll be around. I'm only saying . . . don't ask me for details."

He finished untying her sandals, stood up, and looked again down into her face.

"Boy are you gonna look like your mother! Am I right, Prometheus?"

"Huh? What?" came the answer from the food cupboards. "I'm trying to find something to eat that isn't moving on its own, thank you."

"Oh, just let me do it," said Hermes.

At once the wooden eating table was groaning under the weight of more food than Pandy had ever seen in her life, including feast days.

"Hermes . . . ," said Prometheus.

"Too much?"

"A bit."

"Fine. Ingrate," Hermes said, smiling.

Instantly, much of the food disappeared, but enough was left so no one would go hungry for days. Prometheus and Hermes looked at each other for a moment, then the god and the Titan each gave the other a long hug.

"Thank you, my friend," said Prometheus.

"My pleasure. And I'll think about that thing we talked about on the way down. I'm gone!"

Hermes, with a wink at Pandy, snapped his fingers and he and the magic shoe rack disappeared with a loud crack.

Xander didn't flinch, but Sabina started awake, looking about with a terrified expression. Then smelling the delicious food and realizing where she was, she propelled herself—at a snail's pace—out of the floor pillow and sat down at the table.

"Come on, honey . . . you've got to eat something," said Prometheus to Pandy, feeding Xander a fig.

Just then, Dido wandered in from the courtyard looking dirty and confused, but not any thinner.

"Dido!" Pandy threw her arms around his neck. "C'mere ghost dog. Did you miss me, huh? Hey, hey . . . look at me, Dido. Dad, I think something's wrong with him. He's gotten fatter."

"I've been feeding him," came a small voice from the doorway.

"Iole!" said Pandy.

"Mom and Dad kept turning him away when he started coming to our house for food. So I've been sneaking him some sacrificial leavings and a little rice after everyone goes to sleep."

Iole stood with the sun at her back, but even in silhouette Pandy could tell there was something very wrong. As she got closer, she saw small grayish bumps covering Iole's arms and legs. Then she saw that they were—ever so slightly—wiggling.

"Iole, what happened?" said Pandy, leading her to the table.

"I don't know," Iole said. "But I've been ruminating. I'm pretty sure it's because I was so close to the box when all the vapors and fumes came rushing out. You saw

Helen and Hippia. Well, I was standing just a little farther back and this is what happened. Where have you been?"

"But those plagues aren't supposed to be physical or anything like that; they're just supposed to make people say and do and feel terrible things."

"I think we got it in concentrated form. Where were you?" said Iole.

"Why are they wiggling?" asked Pandy.

Xander had stopped eating and was gaping at Iole's bumps.

"I'm not quite sure," Iole answered. "Pandy, *where* have you been?"

"Do they . . . hurt?" Pandy asked cautiously.

"Oh no. In fact"—Iole suddenly started giggling— "they tickle sometimes. Pandy . . . ?"

"I've been on Mount Olympus," Pandy began, and as she told the story of the map and her quest, the terrible importance of what she'd agreed to do came rushing in upon her. Tears started to well up again.

"You're gonna do it? All by yourself? And you've only got a day to get ready? Let me help you! My parents think I'm off floating in the sulfur baths, trying to get rid of these things. But when Dido started heading for your house, I knew you were back."

"Dad?" said Pandy, turning suddenly. "Why were we gone almost three weeks and I don't remember it?"

"Because," Prometheus said, "you know that Zeus

built his palace on Olympus at a height exactly nine days above the earth, just as the gates of the underworld below us are a nine-day journey from the top of the earth. So it takes exactly nine days to ascend to Olympus from earth and nine days to return. There was no need for you to be awake during the trip, so Morpheus cradled you there and back."

"What was that thing you were talking about with Hermes?"

"What thing?" asked Prometheus.

"The thing that he meant when he said 'I'll think about that thing'?"

"Oh." And he paused. "Pandora, the whole family will suffer if Zeus finds out we helped you in any way. But that doesn't mean I'm not going to keep track of you. I need a way of knowing where and how you are at all times. Hermes is gonna see what he can come up with."

"And another thing . . . Dad, how come you're a Titan and you never told me?"

"Enough questions, Pandora! Eat and then we have to get you ready to . . . go."

Prometheus strode to the doorway, standing for many moments just staring outside. At length, he turned to Sabina.

"Sabina, will you clean the drainage counter and floor, please?"

Sabina glanced up, midbite, with a chicken leg in her mouth. She looked like she was going to say something, but she finished chewing her chicken and got up to find the broom.

"Pandy," said Iole, leaning across the table, "you've got to come see Alcie."

Pandy's heart gave a small lurch. Alcie had actually been standing closer to the opened box than Iole had.

"Why? Gods, what's wrong?"

"She's got two left feet," said Iole.

Pandy didn't get it at first. Okay, Alcie was kinda clumsy, but . . . Then her eyes went wide.

"You mean . . . seriously?"

"Yep. She's been staying in bed a lot. And sitting down. Just basically trying not to *ambulate*."

"What?"

"Um . . . move," Iole said.

"Why?" asked Pandy.

"She keeps going in circles. If she tries to walk through her house she just veers off to the right and crashes into the wall. And something has happened to her mouth . . . kinda."

"Huh?"

"Every once in a while, she says things she doesn't mean . . . or maybe she means them, but she's not thinking before she says them."

"But she's always done that," said Pandy.

"It's worse. And when she's really upset, she keeps mentioning . . . ," Iole said.

"What?" said Pandy.

"Fruit."

"Fru . . . fruit? Gods," said Pandy, standing up. "Dad, I've got to go. I'll be back in a moment."

"You're not leaving this house, young maiden!" he said.

"Dad, Alcie's hurt. And it's my fault. I have to see her. I'll be right back."

And she was already out the door and·running. She paused only briefly to let Iole catch up and then the two girls sprinted over small hills, through woods and olive groves until they reached Alcie's home.

"Go around the back way," said Iole.

"But Alcie's room is in front on the second level."

"She can't climb the stairs. They've put her in a room in the back."

The two friends cautiously made their way around the side of the house and through the garden filled with Alcie's family statues. Pandy, keeping an eye on the windows, accidentally knocked the pinkie finger off Alcie's aunt Aurora, who'd been turned to stone by Medusa. "Oops!" whispered Pandy.

"Oh, Pandy!" said Iole, picking up the finger and waggling it.

Then they started to giggle.

"It's so not funny," said Pandy, trying to stifle herself. "What do I do with it?"

"Put it in her other hand. Maybe they can stick it back on with mortar," said Iole. And the two laughed so hard they had to brace themselves against the other petrified members of Alcie's family until they settled down.

They stifled still more giggles as they rounded the back of the large house and passed quietly underneath two large windows. They came to a small window at the very end of the house and peeked in.

Alcie was lying on a sleeping pallet, propped up with many colorful pillows, a glass of crushed grape juice on a small stand next to her. Her hair was loose around her shoulders and she held a papyrus sheet, trying to write something with a pheasant quill. She looked perfect, like a little goddess; then Pandy looked down the length of the pallet and saw two small feet poking out from under the blanket. Same size, same shape, pointing in exactly the same direction.

"Alcie!" whispered Pandy.

Alcie looked up and saw her two best friends at the window. She smiled for a second and then started to cry.

"Alcie, don't cry, please!" said Pandy. "Can we come in?"

"I . . . guess so. I *hate* your apple entrails, you know!" she said, getting up.

Pandy had started to climb in the window, but Alcie's words stopped her. It was more the tone than the actual words. She means it, Pandy thought. She looked at Iole, who looked back with a nod and a shrug.

Alcie strayed to the right for a bit as she walked to the window, then corrected herself and helped the girls into the room. She sat back on the sleeping pallet with Pandy. Iole stood at the door, listening for anyone approaching.

"When did it happen?" asked Pandy. "You were okay when we all ran away, right?"

"I was fine until the next day. I woke up with a giant pain in my right leg; except it wasn't my right leg anymore. And then I started having major trouble walking, so Mom and Dad are keeping me home from school."

"It's still open?" said Pandy.

"Some of the teachers are there, but not many students," said Iole. "We were pretty close to the source, Pandy; a lot of people are a mess. Damon of Troy, the new kid, has fingernails that won't stop growing. He can't feed himself anymore. Hermia, Hippia's little sister, has two and a half heads. But her house was destroyed, so the family's thinking about going to Rome and putting her in the circus. And Tiresias the Younger is . . . is . . ."

"What? What? What is he?" Pandy said, horrified at what might have befallen her heartthrob.

". . . a girl," said Iole, giggling for a second, then trying to be very serious again.

"Gods, you wretched little . . . tangerine! I can't even wear my best ankle bracelets anymore 'cause they just scrape against each other! Pomegranates! I hope the Colossus of Rhodes falls on your face! May pillars crush you! May . . ." Alcie quickly slapped a hand over her mouth. "I'm . . . I'm sorry."

Pandy was struck dumb again. She paused and knew this couldn't be her best friend talking. Alcie wouldn't be this way if not for her.

"No, listen, Alcie," she said slowly, "it's gonna be okay. I was on Mount Olympus. I'm not kidding. And Zeus said that even though I was terrible and stupid and that he really wanted to do horrible things to my family, he was gonna give me a chance."

As she related the whole story again, Alcie stared at her just the way Iole had.

". . . and Hermes said"—Pandy dropped her voice very low—"that some of them would be around, y'know, kinda watching out and stuff. So don't worry. When I get back . . . I don't know . . . but things will be better. I think. They have to be, right?"

"*If* you get back, you mean, you prune!" Alcie fell back on the pillows with her hand over her mouth again. "I'm sorry, Pandy."

"It's okay, Alcie. Yeah, you're right. If."

Pandy walked to the window, then turned to face her friends: Iole standing guard at the door, her bumps wiggling ever so slightly, and Alcie, unable to walk straight, terrible things coming out of her mouth. This was all her fault, every last bit of it. Then she stood up.

"I'm gonna make this right. I'll try . . . I'll *do* my best, guys. And I'm not gonna mess it up."

Pandy started to climb back out the window.

"You coming, Iole?" she said, looking over her shoulder.

"I'm staying here for a bit."

Pandy paused on the window ledge, realizing that this was probably it; this was good-bye.

"Then I'll see you in . . . I'll see you . . . in six moons."

She jumped back into the room and ran to give Alcie a hug. She motioned for Iole to join them. Iole shook her head and looked ashamedly at her bumps.

"I don't care," whispered Pandy.

Iole wrapped her arms around Pandy and Alcie and the three friends clung to one another for a long, long time.

Then Pandy, certain she'd never see either of them again, climbed out the window and ran back over the hills.

CHAPTER TWELVE

Preparation

When she arrived back home, there were only a few hours of daylight left. She walked in to find the table cleared of all the food conjured by Hermes.

On it instead was a long fur-lined cloak, two hemp sacks, a leather carrying pouch, the map, and a few other items.

"You might have helped us prepare for your departure," called Sabina, storing leftover food at the drainage counter.

"I had to see my friend. She's hurt."

"She's not the only one, my dear," Sabina said, sniffing at an old piece of lamb before tasting it. "Hmm . . . still good."

"Sabina, where's my father? asked Pandy.

"I'm right here, honey."

Prometheus descended the stairway, the wooden box

in one hand and something wrapped in cloth in the other. Pandy walked over and hugged his waist.

"I'm sorry I left, Dad. But Alcie . . . Dad, Alcie and Iole . . ."

"It's fine, sweetheart. Didn't take us long at all. You wouldn't have known where half this stuff was anyway. Come here."

He led her back to the table.

"This pouch should be big enough to hold everything. Now, here is an extra pair of sandals, a clean toga, a spare tooth-rake, and five sticks of Sabina's lavender-cinnamon chewing sap."

"She never gives that away!"

"She cares about you, daughter . . . and she wanted to give you a little comfort. Besides, it's starting to pull her teeth out. Now," he said, holding up the smaller pouch, which jingled a little, "this is extra money for food and supplies. Sabina is packing you some dried foods, which should last a long time, but you'll run out sooner or later. Save this money as long as you can, though."

Pandy looked at Sabina, now inhaling the scent from a plate of moldy olives, and remembered her seconds earlier, sniffing at the lamb. She made a furious mental note to check all the provisions before she left the house.

"Here's your food sack," her father continued, packing

all of the items into the leather pouch. "Your water-skin, and the map, and finally, the box."

"What's this?" said Pandy, holding up the cloak. "I mean, I know what it is, but whose is it?"

Prometheus gazed at the cloak.

"This was . . . is . . . your mother's. It's the first present I gave to her after we were married. I guess it's a little shabby for her now; she never wears it anymore. But the fur is still thick and it will keep you warm. Don't mind the length, you can tuck it into your girdle if it drags a little."

"Dad," she said, looking down at her belt, "my training girdle will never be able to hold that cloak."

"Right," he said, then he paused and held out the cloth bundle. "Right you are, daughter. And so I have also decided to give you this . . ."

Pandora unwrapped her mother's silver girdle.

Like a wave washing over her, she felt every emotion leave her but despair. She was flooded with it, then with anger at herself, and then terrible, terrible fear. She realized that the moment she put on her mother's girdle, the days of being an irresponsible girl were gone . . . forever. She clung to her father and sobbed for so long that it was only Sabina's voice, muttering something about how green cheese could still be good cheese, that brought her back.

"Pandora, why don't you go play with your little

brother," Prometheus said. "He won't be so little when . . . when you come home."

She couldn't think of anything, at that moment, that she wanted to do more. She nodded and raced upstairs to Xander's room.

"After evening meal you and I will examine the map," Prometheus called after her.

"Okay!"

She found Xander on the floor, trying to eat the glass-bead eye off of his stuffed Cyclops.

"Hey, you . . . ," she said softly, settling down next to him and tickling his tail. "Whatcha doing, there? Huh?"

Xander looked at her, suspiciously at first; he'd become used to his big sister ignoring him, and his little tail fanned out in hesitation. But after a moment, he handed her the doll, which she started to play with. Xander giggled madly at his big sister's antics with the one-eyed furball. He ran around his room finding other toys and dolls, carefully and meticulously explaining each and every one of them to Pandy. They all enjoyed a pretend feast, which became a war, which became a dance, which became a race, which became a shopping spree, which finally became a slumber party when Xander passed out.

Pandy lay down next to him. She looked at him sleeping peacefully next to his Hercules doll. When she came home, she vowed, she was gonna do this more often. She promised him. She promised herself.

"Evening meal!" called Sabina.

"Already?" said Pandy, coming downstairs.

"Well, you didn't eat anything earlier," said Prometheus.

She had completely forgotten, realizing she was famished.

"Besides, I want you on your pallet early," he said. "You must get as much sleep as you can."

Pandy sat down to a huge meal of chicken, rice, hummus, flatbread, boiled vegetables, and honey cakes. She cleaned her plate and asked for another.

When she'd finally had enough, her father brought out the yellowed sheepskin bag from the pouch. He started to untie the golden string when Pandy stopped him.

"Dad, let me. Just in case no one is supposed to touch it but me."

He smiled and handed the bag to her. Pandy loosed the string, broke the seal of Hera, and slowly unfolded the soft sheepskin.

Inside was a small blue marble bowl. The outside was divided, top to bottom, in three concentric rings, each of varying dark blue shades in comparison to the light blue marble inside. Each ring had a series of seven groups of strange symbols circling the bowl. Pandy recognized only a few of the symbols as numbers and letters.

"This is a map?" she said.

"It must be."

"How do I read it?" she asked.

"It's a bowl . . . let's put something in it," said Prometheus.

They filled the bowl with goat's milk and stared for a few minutes into the murky whiteness.

"Nothing, Dad!" said Pandy.

They filled the bowl with water, grape juice, honey, olive oil, wine, lemon juice, and cream. All in vain.

"Maybe it's not a liquid," said Pandy.

They tried grapes, figs, cheese, garlic cloves, basil leaves, lentils—everything in the food cupboards. Nothing yielded any result.

"Pandora," said Prometheus. "Let's think about this. The map is supposed to be able to be used anywhere. What's one of the most common substances?"

"Water? But we tried that, Dad."

"I know. I know. But let's do it again."

They rinsed the bowl and filled it again with fresh water. Then they stared at it. And stared at it.

Pandora didn't know how long it would be till the sky darkened, but she knew they were wasting precious time with this stupid bowl. She was going to leave in the morning and never return, she was sure of it. But she was determined to be brave, so when her tears started to fall, she didn't shake or sniffle. She just let them roll down her cheeks and off her chin, splashing onto the table.

All except one.

One tear missed the wooden table where the others had landed and splashed into the water.

At once the rings on the outside of the bowl began to turn left and right, crossing over each other again and again. At last, three symbols, three distinct words in Greek, lined up with one another from the top ring to the bottom and radiated a bright blue light.

"Tears, Pandora!" said Prometheus. "The map works with your tears!"

"Great. I have to be crying all the time," she said, reaching up to brush the remaining tears away.

"Stop! Don't touch them!" said her father. Prometheus hurried to the drainage counter and found a small glass vial. He laid it carefully against his daughter's cheek, catching five large tears inside.

"That's a start," he said, corking the vial tightly. "You can use these if you keep the air out."

"Thanks, Dad."

"Maybe it's a good thing not to be so brave sometimes," he said. "Now, let's see what we're dealing with."

Delphi read the word on the top ring. The city was the site of the famous Oracle of Apollo and the high priestess who knew all and told all, good and bad. The oracle was the destination for those who wanted to know what their future held.

Underneath, on the middle ring, was the number

180. In fact, that number was the only symbol on the ring at all.

And the bottom ring radiated a single word.

Jealousy.

"That's where you have to go first, Pandora," Prometheus said, pointing past her a little to the north and a little to the west. "That way."

"Dad," she blurted, truly starting to panic. "How am I going to be able to read the rest of the map? How do I capture anything when I get . . . wherever I have to go?"

Prometheus uncorked the vial and caught a few more of her tears and then he took Pandy by the shoulders. He began slowly, unsure where his words would take him, but needing to say something that would comfort his child.

"Listen very carefully, Pandora. I know you saw that fountain in the great hallway on Olympus. You asked me about it then, but *then* was not the best time. Now is."

He paused.

"You know that I am one of the immortals . . . ageless, and endowed with certain powers. But what you don't know, because I've never told you, is that I am actually a Titan . . . created before the great gods of Olympus. When the world was very young we, my brothers and sisters and I, were basically the only beings on the earth, except for a few monsters and a couple of Cyclops. Then, my brother Cronus and his wife, Rhea, rulers of the sky and earth, gave birth to the great gods. But Cronus didn't want any of his children to live because he'd been foretold that one of them would defeat him and become supreme ruler. So he ate them, all of them, except one boy that Rhea hid away."

"Zeus?"

"Right. And when Zeus was old enough, he fought his father for supremacy. Now we—all the Titans— knew the prophecy. Zeus was going to win, plain and simple. So even though the rest of my brothers and sisters decided 'prophecy-shmophecy' and fought against Zeus, I sided with him, because, well . . . basically I wanted to stay alive. After the battle, Zeus rewarded me by not sending me down into the pits of Tartarus or giving me something like the weight of the world to bear upon my shoulders for eternity."

"Uncle Atlas?"

"Right again. Why don't we have the rest of the family over for feast days? It's because they're all chained up in a pit deep in the earth. But Zeus bestowed great favors upon me. I became even more cunning and shrewd. That's why Hermes and I are such good friends. I was clever before, but after the battle I was even smarter. Able to figure almost anything out with enough time . . . except maybe your mother."

"Dad . . . ," Pandy blurted, ". . . you've done all this wonderful stuff, you've seen everything and . . . and you're really strong and now . . . your job . . . now you . . . you . . ."

"Build atriums? Is that it? Why do I do that for a living instead of chasing down Hydras and Chimeras or something like that?"

Pandy shrugged.

"It's simple, Pandora. I fell in love and married your mother. When you were on the way, I realized that I needed to find something more suitable for a family man to keep me occupied. And then, of course, I took one look at my baby girl and knew I couldn't be off risking my life when you and your mother and then Xander were depending on me. Also, your mother . . . well, she didn't like all the attention I got . . . being a hero."

"She didn't want anyone else to get any attention, you mean," said Pandy.

"Stop it, Pandora," he said softly. "Don't forget, your mother was courted by the bravest and noblest young heroes. She could have had anyone, you know. She tries hard to be a good . . . She fails a lot, but she tries. Look, Pandora, I do what I do for the same reason I married your mother. I love it. I laid the groundwork for the Pyramids. I poured the first casting of the Colossus of Rhodes. I hung the first basket of hydrangeas after building the Hanging Gardens of Babylon. Sure, Zeus has me ignite the odd extinct volcano now and then, when he wants to lay waste to this or that city. It's fun and a good chance to travel. But basically, I build things; it's what I *do* . . . and it gives me great pleasure. Only now I do it on a smaller scale so I can be with my family. People will always need atriums. I just build them in fun, clever ways . . . no one else but your dad can cleverly weld decorative ironwork with their hands . . . it's my trademark. Which brings me back to my point. In addition to heightening my brainpower, cunning, and shrewdness, Zeus promised me that these traits would pass down to my family. That's why, Pandora, even though I am absolutely despondent about what you've done, deep down I am not surprised. It was just too tempting."

She stared at her dad.

"And since you've become a maiden, I have no doubt that your powers will start developing."

"What powers, Dad? Iole was talking about them, too."

"The power to think things through, to see the big picture, not just the small scene. To use your wonderful mind to its absolute fullest. And don't forget, sweetheart, you're semi-immortal . . . so the power of your mind might manifest itself in interesting ways. You'll be able to figure out this map. You'll ask, you'll ponder, you'll learn."

"Me being semi-immortal . . . is that what kept me from being harmed by the box like Alcie and Iole?"

"No, that was Zeus," her father replied.

"What?"

"Hermes told me. Zeus didn't want you feeling any ill effects until and unless he inflicted them."

"Gods. Then I really need to thank Hera again tonight."

"Yes," Prometheus said thoughtfully. "Yes . . . well . . . don't count on anything more from heaven's queen. She's a bit like your mother that way . . . she can be generous, but there's usually a price."

"Huh?"

"Never mind," he answered.

Pandy started crying again.

"Dad, I didn't mean to get Mom turned into a pile of ashes!"

"I know you didn't, sweetheart," Prometheus said, uncorking the vial of tears again and holding it against her face.

"I know we aren't really getting along so good . . . ," Pandy said. "That is, when she's even home, but I miss her. I don't know why she doesn't love me anymore, but I'm not just going away so Zeus won't chain us in a pit. I'm doing it for Mom, too. You know that, right?"

"Of course I know that. And don't ever think your mother doesn't love you. The truth is this, Pandora, you're not a little girl anymore and she's having trouble adjusting to you becoming such a grown-up young maiden. I know it reminds her that she's not getting any younger. Your mother was and still is one of the most beautiful women in all of Greece, but seeing you . . . well, she's just a little insecure. But believe me, somewhere on Olympus there's a pile of ashes in an urn that loves you very much."

Pandy had never thought of her mother as anything other than cool and strong; the fact that her mother didn't feel confident and self-assured all the time never occurred to her. She thought of her mother's urn, seeing it sitting on the great teardrop table, and hoped it was being kept safe and warm.

"Okay," Prometheus said, corking the vial, "off to sleep. I'll be up in a minute to kiss you good night."

Pandy looked once more at the things they had gathered. She took her mother's silver girdle and walked upstairs for what she knew would be the last safe night in a long time.

In her room, Pandy just stood for many minutes, staring without really seeing anything. Then her sleeping pallet came into focus with Dido snoring peacefully on top. She looked hard at her writing desk and her small chair. Then she gazed at her fire grate and the embers giving off soothing warmth. Pandy picked up a piece of hot, glowing wood. Tossing it back into the grate, she began to touch everything else around her. She climbed her wooden shelves, running her hands over old, outgrown togas and forgotten accessories. She touched each piece of wood, every bump in the clay walls, the wood of her soiled-toga basket . . .

Gods!

She'd put her lunch in it the day of the project almost three weeks ago! She cautiously approached and lifted the lid, expecting it to be full of crawly things.

Instead, the basket was empty except for a small scrap of papyrus.

This is not the drainage counter. When you come home, please deposit your food in the proper receptacle.

Sabina

Addendum: Look after yourself.

Suddenly she couldn't look at everything fast enough. She knew she should be sleeping, but her whole world was going to be terrifyingly different starting at daybreak and she wanted to sear this moment in her memory; something she could call on to cover her like a soft blanket in the days ahead.

CHAPTER THIRTEEN

Dear Diary

"Dear Diary . . . ."

"Blessed you are among mortals. Good evening, Pandora. What do you have to tell me?" said the wolf head, then added, "As if I didn't know. And I do, so don't even think about telling me the whole thing again."

"How do you know?"

"I hear things. You think I'm only alert when you talk, but I'm not. I see things, too. And the Huntress speaks to me. She was here earlier, before you came in."

"Artemis was here? In my room?"

"Yes, Pandora. She left a message for you. In all of my years with you, this will be the first time that I have given advice, but as it comes from the great one herself, I do it gladly."

"What is it?"

"You are to take me with you," said the wolf.

"Why?"

"You dare question the goddess who, out of love and respect for your father, his selflessness and torment, gave me to you? A diary . . . a record keeper the likes of which no other maiden has?"

"No . . . it's only . . . where will I keep you? My pouch is full and I . . ."

"Astonishing! Still thinking only about you. Make room, Pandora!"

"Yes, yes, of course. I'm sorry," she muttered.

"Good. Now don't roll me up; lay me flat in front of your fire grate. I'd like to be warm tonight, if you please."

Pandy unfolded the skin and put it in front of the fire. Dido immediately got off the pallet and plopped himself down right on top.

"Yes . . . well," the wolfskin panted, "this was unexpected. Is he going to lie here all night? Get off!"

Dido didn't move.

"Oh, well, just fine. I'm very warm now, thanks," said the skin. "What *has* this dog been eating?"

"I was wondering . . . ," Pandy said. "Could you tell Dido a little bit of the story? I know he's been worried, and . . ."

"Yes, of course. Why on earth would I need to sleep, hmm?"

"Thank you. Good night, then," said Pandy.

"Good night, daughter of Prometheus." The wolfskin sounded as if all the air had been sucked out of it.

"Sleep well in the arms of Morpheus. Blessed are you among mortals."

Pandy put on her sleeping robes. She threw her training girdle into the wastebasket, knowing she would never wear it again. Lying on her pallet she listened to the wolfskin making soft whining noises and Dido answering with gulps and whimpers. There were a thousand things she should be taking instead of her diary. Who would ever want to know what she was going to go through? She'd probably end up lost forever in a cave or on a mountaintop before the cycle of seasons had passed anyway.

She lay awake for a long time imagining impossible terrors, but finally, just as she began to doze, she felt a light kiss and the soft brush of her father's beard on her forehead.

Oh yes, Pandy thought, Dad always kisses me good night. That's the way it always is. Always will be.

And she slept.

Prometheus sat at the large table in the family living space, alternately gazing through the window at the night sky and looking down at a small oval disc in his hand. It was a marble and black onyx carving of Pandy when she was about six years old, just her profile. He remembered a little girl sitting on the edge of the catch basin in the lavatorium watching him use his shaving blade and making him laugh so hard by asking him all sorts of silly questions that he had to pause every so often before he brought the blade to his neck. What he wouldn't give to have her that age and size again, just staring at him adoringly as he shaved.

He scanned the darkness for any sign that Apollo was preparing to draw the sun through the sky.

"It won't be light anytime soon," whispered a voice from behind his chair. "Besides, there's a big . . . shall we say, *discussion* going on up at home, and until we get a few things resolved, daybreak will just have to wait."

"I was beginning to give up on you," said Prometheus.

"Were you really? Nice. Very nice. Doubting a god, my friend? I'm crushed," said Hermes.

"What happened to the bright lights?" said Prometheus. "I thought you were under orders to shine."

"That's when I'm on the clock, bringing news or messages, edicts, pronouncements, and that sort of thing, blah, blah, blah. Not when I'm on my own time, bringing you this."

Hermes withdrew from the folds of his toga a small green silk bag.

"What is it?"

"Well, open it, for my sake!"

Prometheus laid the bag on the table and loosened

the thin yellow cord. Inside were two small conch shells, each about the size of an average lemon. Prometheus held one in his hand, turning it gently. "Hold it up to your ear," said Hermes.

Prometheus did so and looked at Hermes.

"Nothing . . . ," Prometheus said after a moment.

"Oh, right! Someone has to be on the other end. Okay, put it down on the table and when it rattles, pick it up and listen. Hang on."

Hermes snatched up the other shell and disappeared in a quiet puff of silver smoke.

After a number of seconds, Prometheus was starting to feel silly staring at the shell when he heard a slight rattling sound coming out of it. He quickly put the conch to his ear and heard Hermes' voice; it was higher pitched, but as clear as if he'd been in the room.

"Come in, Athens. Calling out to Athens. Athens, come in!"

"Hermes? Where are you?"

"I can barely hear you, pal. Put the shell to your mouth when you want to say something," said Hermes.

Prometheus took the shell from his ear and spoke into it directly.

"Where are you?" he said again, then put the conch quickly back to his ear.

"Mesopotamia!"

"I can hear you! I can hear you!" said Prometheus.

"And that, my friend, is the whole idea," came a voice again from behind his chair.

Prometheus realized exactly what this meant.

"Hermes! You wouldn't lie to me. Were you really in . . . ? Were you really so far away?" he began. "It's . . . it's not that I'm doubting you. It's just that . . . that . . . this means I can . . ."

He sat down again and was silent, staring up at the god.

Hermes knelt by his friend, putting a huge hand on his shoulder.

"I would have brought you a little water from the Euphrates, but I wanted to get back."

"I can talk to her, Hermes? Tomorrow, when she's on her way to Delphi? Wherever she is, I'll be able to talk to her?" said Prometheus, a tremor in his voice.

"Rather fantastic, am I right? Uncle Poseidon brought the shells from the shores of some island or other, and Athena took them and made with the hocus-pocus. Now they're yours. Whenever Pandora wants to talk, you'll hear a small rattle. Or if you want silence, just run your finger straight down along the lip of the shell and then it will vibrate ever so slightly with no noise. However, there's a catch."

"Well of course, there had to be, didn't there?" Prometheus said, slumping.

"It's not that bad. They just don't work well in the mountains. There's a lot of interference. Also, Zeus may be monitoring her closely for a little while, so don't use the shells too frequently. Use them at night, or if it's really cloudy. Be discreet. Because, let me tell you, if he finds out that anyone in my family is aiding her in any way . . . what he'll do to us will make what he was going to do to you look like a picnic in the Elysian Fields."

Prometheus's eyes lit up.

"Hermes! Are the others in on this? Not just you?"

"Pal, the less you know, the better. Let me put it this way: you can worry, just not as much. All right?"

Prometheus threw his arms about Hermes and almost knocked the wind out of him.

"Thank you, my friend."

"Yeah, well, don't go dancing around a fire pit yet, pal. Okay, I am so late. Be smart with the shells. I'm gone!"

And he was.

Prometheus picked up one of the shells and tucked it into the leather carrying pouch. He glanced over the table to make sure nothing had been forgotten. Then he ascended the stairs, moving past his children's curtained rooms until he parted his own red privacy curtain and lay down to catch what little sleep he could.

CHAPTER FOURTEEN
The Meeting

High on Mount Olympus, Artemis followed Hermes down a long, dimly lit flight of marble stairs to a darkened suite of rooms.

"Why are you so late?" she asked.

"I was delivering something to Prometheus," Hermes answered. "Just an informal communication device for father and daughter. What about you?"

"I was giving some last-minute instructions to her diary. Why are we doing this down here?" She shuddered.

"Because," said her brother, moving deeper into the mountain, "no one ever uses Hades' apartments, especially when he's not here, so this is the last place Hera will think to look."

None of the immortals ever wanted to linger in Hades' suite. The Lord of the Underworld demanded no windows and very little light, so his rooms were sunk into the heart of Mount Olympus. One wall was made from the skulls of cowards who'd fled the battlefield; the mortar holding them together was mixed with bone marrow. Another wall looked perfectly normal, but if it was touched in any way, it sounded the scream of a million souls in torment. Yet another wall was simply a cascade of red acid. Privacy curtains were made of long strands of the back molars of murderers all strung together. Scattered about were strange and terrifying artifacts Hades had collected over the centuries as God of the Dead: dinosaur bones, glass jars of round Etruscan blood beads, pots of smoke, and floor rugs made of human hairs. And Hades never, ever permitted anyone into his sleeping chamber. Because that's where the real horror was: his private collection of clown frescoes and pressed-flower scrapbooks.

"What if she discovers us?" asked Artemis.

"Aphrodite and Dionysus have it all worked out," Hermes continued, walking swiftly through a gloomy sitting room. "Ares is standing guard, and if he sees or hears anything, we all switch to plan beta."

Before Artemis could ask what, exactly, plan beta was, they arrived at a small silver door. Hermes knocked twice and then twice again. The door opened a crack and Artemis could just make out Ares' yellow eyes before he swung wide the door and almost yanked them into the room.

Around a low table lit only by a single candle sat Aphrodite, Apollo, Athena, Poseidon, Dionysus, Demeter, and Hephaestus. Eros was asleep on a cushioned couch in the corner.

"Where's Uncle Hades?" Artemis asked, sitting down and laying her hunting bow beside her chair.

"Oh, please," said Poseidon, adjusting the several large wet strips of cotton keeping his tail moist. "My brother couldn't care less about this whole mess. He deals with grief and sorrows by the cartload every day in the underworld. You think this bothers him? He's amused, actually. Told me so."

"That's sick," said Aphrodite.

"That's Hades," said Athena.

"By the way, where's Zeus?" asked Demeter.

"I told him there was a group of gorgeous young things skinny-dipping off of the islands of Delos, so he turned himself into a shark and went for a swim," said Hermes.

Ares piped up, "And when he gets there and no one is skinny-dipping, smarty?"

"Oh, they're there, all right. A few friends owed me some favors, so I'm having them splash about for a bit."

The gods stared at Hermes in disbelief.

"Hey!" he said. "I told him the truth . . . they're things. Tails, scales, fins, you name it."

"And I'm keeping the water churning, so Zeus won't be able to make anything out for quite a while," offered Poseidon, squeezing a sea sponge over his head.

"What about 'she who must be feared'?" said Hephaestus.

"I sorta let the same info slip to Hera," said Hermes. " 'Zeus is leering at pretty young things . . . again.' She took off like a vulture, slow moving but deadly."

"Okay, let's get to it," said Apollo. "Who's going to help Pandora with what? Hephaestus, you've got Jealousy, right?"

"Right," Hephaestus said, shifting his sooty little body in his chair. "What I planned to do was—"

"Wait just a tick or two on the sundial, if you please," said Demeter. "Before Artemis and Hermes came in, I believe I was asking why Hera hates Pandora so much and what she thinks she is going to gain by sending this poor little maiden all over creation on a wild plague chase. So will somebody, in plain Greek, please explain it to me?"

"Okay, okay . . . very quickly, here's the deal," said Apollo. "Three years ago, both Pandora and Hera's great-granddaughter, Ariadne of Calydon, were involved in Aphrodite's Girl/Goddess Guides. Different chapters, but the same organization."

"Makes me sorry I ever started the whole thing," said Aphrodite quietly.

"Not your fault, sister," said Apollo. "So the group needed to raise funds for . . . whatever, and they decided to sell sacks of oatie cakes. The humans in charge thought, hey, why not make a little contest out of it?

The girl who sold the most sacks won . . . what was it again, Aphrodite?"

"A makeover with me," she said, hanging her head.

"A makeover?" slurred Dionysus. "They're children!"

"Anyway," Apollo said, "wherever they could—at the markets, alongside the chariot roads, in front of the temples, door to door, you name it—the girls were there, hawking the cakes. Now, because Ariadne is Hera's great-granddaughter, she was selling hundreds of sacks. Hera was conning all of the immortals into buying ox-carts full of the things!"

"Honeyed oatie cakes, lemon oatie cakes, oatie cakes with dried grapes!" moaned Athena, she and her owl both rolling their eyes.

"I've still got sacks full in my storage rooms," said Artemis. "I give them to my temple priestesses to hand out to people who pray really hard . . . or not."

"I use them as fish food," said Poseidon.

"Kindling," said Hephaestus. "They burn great on the forge."

"I've sent a million sacks down to Egypt," said Dionysus. "They ran out of bricks for the Pyramids."

"Although, and I think we'll all agree," Aphrodite chimed in, "when it's hot, there's nothing better than a carob-covered mint oatie cake right off an ice block . . ."

"So Ariadne was in the lead for a long time," Apollo continued. "But Pandora is Prometheus's daughter and, let's face it, he basically saved the human race. When people found out that his kid wanted a few drachmas for a sack or two, the orders couldn't be filled fast enough. So at the last moment, Pandora ends up winning and Hera's great-granddaughter lost."

"And Pandora got the makeover?" asked Dionysus.

"Pandora's mother said no," Aphrodite replied. "She wanted to test the products on herself first and see what was fit for her daughter. Pandora was only ten years old then and oh, she was so excited. She only wanted to be like her mother. My heart just broke. I wanted to turn Sybilline into a boar, but Zeus told me not to interfere."

"And that's the story," said Apollo.

There was a long silence.

"You have got to be kidding me, right? This is a joke!" Demeter said at length. "Hera's still angry because her great-granddaughter lost?"

"Well, Ariadne could use a makeover," Aphrodite muttered.

"You should have seen Hera," said Hephaestus. "She wanted to level Prometheus's house."

"Athens. She wanted to destroy Athens," said Athena.

"I know Hera is petty, mean-spirited, envious, nasty, and thoughtless, but come on," said Demeter.

"She's never forgiven Pandora," said Apollo. "So now that she's opened the box, this is a chance not only to get even, but to punish and probably kill her as well."

"Then why give her the map?" asked Demeter, twirling her wheat-grass hair. "Is it fake?"

"No," said Athena. "I know Zeus saw it before Hera wrapped it up, so she couldn't completely toy with Pandora. It shows all the locations of the plagues, but it is very difficult to decipher. Look, we know that Pandora's only got a limited amount of time. She has find everything within six moons."

There was another long pause.

"What happens, again . . . if it goes beyond that?" asked Dionysus, unusually quiet.

"Yeah, what happens if she doesn't succeed?" asked Artemis.

"Evil stays put. Everything that's still out of the box is permanent. No getting it back. Done. Finished," breathed Ares out of his helmet mouth hole. "Kinda helps my business . . ."

Everyone looked at him.

"Just saying," he said.

"It's much more than that now," Aphrodite spoke up. "Hera has become the embodiment of everything in that box. She's jealous, greedy, vain . . . you name it! What will happen is this: she'll wipe out mankind."

"What?" gasped Artemis.

"She will. Ultimately," Aphrodite continued. "If evil becomes permanent, she will harness each plague to her own selfish purposes and with that much power, fueled by all that hatred, she will be able to destroy everything in her path. Men first, as punishment for Zeus never being faithful. Women next, because any woman is a threat. Mankind, as it is, will cease to exist."

"Um . . . hang on just a moment, if you please," said Dionysus. "If mankind is gone . . . then who . . . who . . . ?"

"Go ahead, Uncle. Say it," said Apollo.

"Who will believe in . . . us?" Dionysus said slowly.

No one spoke.

Hermes cleared his throat. "If Pandora fails," he said, "then mankind will be eradicated from the face of the earth. We will become shadows . . . and simply fade away."

"Great Gods . . . ," said Hephaestus, after a pause.

"No. We won't be. If we're lucky, Hera will just chain our spirits in Tartarus to keep us out of the way," said Hermes.

"That's if we're lucky. My guess is, she'll create a whole new species of beings. Devoted to her . . . made in her image. But she'll destroy first the things she hates the most," said Poseidon.

"Will she start with herself?" asked Ares.

"Could Zeus do anything?" asked Dionysus, now quite sober.

"With that much evil in her hands, even Zeus, more powerful than all of us together, will be like a deer in the jaws of a lion," Apollo said.

Silence fell again as each of the gods weighed the significance of Apollo's words.

"Pandora must be helped whenever and wherever possible," said Hermes.

"But subtly," said Athena.

"And that's where we come in," said Ares, punching one fist into the other.

"Right," said Apollo. "Each of us gives her a little assistance on the sly when she's going after whatever we originally put in the box. So, where were we? Jealousy? Hephaestus, whatcha got?"

"Okay. Well, since Jealousy . . . Envy . . . Covetousness . . . call it what you will, was my contribution, and I think we all know *why*"—he paused to stare straight at Aphrodite and Ares—"I forged a small net made of a gold-adamant alloy. It's absolutely unbreakable and inescapable. With this she'll be able to capture everything."

"Excellent," said Apollo. "Where's she off to first? Hermes?"

"Delphi."

"Oh, that's just great. The site of my temple and my oracle. Well, I can't get involved there. Hera will be on the lookout and she'll run to tell Zeus. So I have to hang back. But I can help with Vanity, when she gets to it."

"I'm still surprised that something you think is so normal about yourself is the thing you chose to curse mankind," giggled Aphrodite.

"Don't make me come across this table," said Apollo.

"My twin brother and I went in on Vanity together, Aphrodite, so if you're going to insult him . . . ," said Artemis, reaching for her great bow.

"Children, children, please," said Athena. "Greed was mine, so I have that one."

One by one the gods claimed their respective evils: Aphrodite would help with Lust, Dionysus with Laziness, and Ares with Rage. Demeter had put in a few lesser evils like depression, acne, migraines, loneliness, excessive homework, "cooties," taking things for granted, lovers' disinterest, and a piggish desire for cherry-vanilla ice cream.

"You keep telling us what ice cream is; however, I don't get the concept," said Athena.

"Just an idea; still working on it," Demeter replied.

"Uncle Poseidon . . . what did you put in?" asked Hermes.

"Don't you remember? I had just sunk those ungrateful, arrogant Atlantians that day and I was all soggy, so I kept flooding the box. All the red, yellow, and black smoke kept fizzling out. Besides, you kids had everything pretty much covered. Don't worry though, I'll help where I can."

"That just leaves the big one," said Apollo. "Fear."

"And that was Hera's," said Ares.

Another long silence.

"Bright ideas, anyone? I'm open to bright ideas," said Apollo.

"Look, we've got it worked out for at least a few weeks, right?" said Dionysus. "Let's see where we are when she gets to it. No stress, okay? Who wants wine?"

Suddenly Ares went rigid.

"Quiet!" he commanded.

In the hush, no one even breathed.

From somewhere in Hades' apartments came the sound of footsteps; heavy, but sporadic, as if a very large body were trying to tiptoe around a room.

Instantly, Aphrodite waved her hand and a large banner appeared overhead that read "Happy Birthday, Hera!" and several samples of cakes materialized on the table.

Dionysus snapped his fingers and dozens of small casks of wine appeared next to the cakes and the gods found themselves each with a full goblet.

Hephaestus grabbed the golden net, quickly hiding it in the folds of his grimy toga as Aphrodite began speaking in an overly loud voice.

"This banner is lovely. Of course, on the night of the party, it'll be large enough to cover the entire great hall."

Ares nodded, then picked up a goblet just as the door flew open and Hera, her mouth clenched and her brows knit into a scowl, filled the doorway.

"Aha! The halls are empty and you all are plotting . . . and . . . planning . . . sending me away . . . wild nymph chase . . ."

Then her jaw dropped.

"Huh?"

The gods gave a tremendous jump as if they had been engrossed, and looked at Hera with their best disappointed faces.

". . . it's last year's vintage from Corinth. It's woodsy and fruity. You can really taste the oak and blackberries. It's perfect for her birthday," Dionysus said.

"What?" gaped Hera.

"Oh! You! Here! Well, that's just terrific," said Aphrodite, starting to cry. "Party ruined, thank you so much! And after all the trouble we've gone through."

"Who couldn't keep a secret, that's what I want to know? Who talked?" asked Apollo, looking around.

"Is this for me?" asked Hera sweetly.

"Oh, I can't bear it. It was going to be the loveliest party. I . . . just . . . can't . . . bear . . ." And with that, Aphrodite ran sobbing from the room.

"I'll go after her. Poor thing, her heart's broken, and you know how rare that is for her!" said Athena, rising.

"I'll come with you," said Demeter, dashing out the door.

"Me too!" said Artemis.

"She probably needs me right about now," said Ares.

"Maybe she needs her *husband*, did you ever think of that, you bloodthirsty mongrel?" said Hephaestus, reaching the doorway with Ares, the two gods trying to squeeze through at the same time.

"Well, I'll just toss these cake samples if we're not going to use them," said Hermes.

"What do you mean, you're *not* going to use them?" screeched Hera. "All right, so I spoiled the surprise . . . but that doesn't mean we can't have a party, right?"

"You'll have to talk to Aphrodite 'bout that," said Hermes, vanishing with the cakes.

"Apollo?" Hera clutched at his golden breastplate. "Apollo, we can still have a party, right? When was it going to be? I'll act surprised, I promise. I will!"

"Sorry, Hera . . . the fun just seems to have gone out of it now."

Apollo hung his head low and sighed very, very deeply. He was about to walk out of the room when he noticed Dionysus downing the third of several small goblets of wine. Apollo picked him up by the neck of his toga and led him through the door.

"Come, Uncle," said Apollo, "it's time we got you to bed."

"Sounds good. Let me just get my goblet . . ."

"No. No more for you," said Apollo, leading Dionysus down the dark hallway. "Good night, Hera. Maybe next year. Sleep well."

And they were gone, leaving Hera alone with a banner and several casks of wine.

"I'd act surprised!" she called after them. "I would!"

She sat down at the low table.

"I really would."

CHAPTER FIFTEEN
Starting Out

Pandy awoke just as Apollo dragged the sun free of the horizon line and a light wind wafted over the city.

She came downstairs, dressed in her clean, white, "good company" toga and wearing her mother's silver girdle, her hair swept back in the tortoiseshell clip. Dido was at her heels and she carried the wolfskin diary under her arm. She felt ages older than when she had gone to sleep and was trying her best to manage a big, happy smile.

Sabina was puttering at the drainage counter while her father and Xander waited for her at the table.

"Good morning, Dad. Good morning, Sabina."

"Good morning, daughter," answered Prometheus.

"Pandeee!" squealed Xander.

"Hi, cutie," she said, cupping his little face and rubbing her nose against his, which caused him to break into peals of laughter.

"This is for you," said Sabina setting down a plate of roasted chicken, boiled eggs, oatie cakes, and honey.

"Eggs . . . my favorite. Thank you, Sabina."

"They'll give you a good start, if nothing else . . . ," Sabina replied, her voice trailing off. Pandy looked up as Sabina turned back toward the food cupboards and noticed a single tear falling down the old woman's cheek.

"Thank you, Sabina," said Prometheus.

There was a charged silence as Pandy ate her morning meal.

"Dad, you're staring at me," she finally said.

"Can you blame me? Besides, you're beginning to look like your mother."

"Puh-leeze."

"You'll probably be her mirror image when you get back," said her father.

"*If* I get back, you mean."

"Don't speak like that!" said Prometheus with such force both Xander and Pandy jumped. Xander was on the verge of tears until his father relaxed his frown and reached out for Pandy.

Pandy finished her morning meal with one hand; with the other, she clung tight to her father.

Finally Prometheus drew the leather carrying pouch across the table and pulled out the conch shell.

"This is the most important thing you'll be carrying,"

he said, lowering his head, speaking very softly. Pandy stared into his face.

"This is a gift from . . . someone. I have the mate in my room. With this, you and I will be able to talk to each other, Pandora. Wherever you are."

"What?" whispered Pandy.

Prometheus repeated all of Hermes' instructions and warnings.

"In fact," said Prometheus, running his finger down the lip of the conch, "let's not take any chances, shall we? We'll just set it to vibrate and no one will be the wiser."

"Does it really work, Dad?"

"Honey, trust me. But be careful."

"Let's have a signal," Pandy said.

"A signal?"

"Sure, if you call and I can't talk, I'll say something like 'The winged horse flies at midnight.'"

"And if you call and I can't talk," said Prometheus, "although I strongly doubt that will ever happen, I'll say, 'Sabina made a wonderful meal.'"

Pandy broke into a huge grin.

"Then I'll know things are really bad back here," she said, then paused. "Oh, Daddy . . ."

"Honey . . . ," he began, but at that instant there was an enormous crack of thunder overhead.

"She's going," he said loudly but respectfully, staring

skyward, his hand covering the conch shell. "Come on, no time to waste."

He stood up, and quickly slipping the shell inside the pouch, began to fasten it shut.

"Wait, Dad . . . I have to put something else in there."

She put her diary inside; by now the pouch was bulging, but it still shut easily.

Pandy knelt and kissed Xander on the cheek. She went to the food cupboards, where Sabina was gazing quietly out the window and threw her arms about the old, old woman's waist. Pandy felt a bony hand clasp her arm tightly, but Sabina didn't turn around. Then Pandy put on her mother's cloak and fastened it inside her girdle. She threw the leather pouch and water-skin crossways over her shoulder, looked around the house once, and walked out the door.

Her father walked with her through the inner court-yard to the small door in the wall surrounding the house. Dido came bounding out to follow her and Prometheus grabbed him by the scruff to keep him back. Pandy patted her dog quickly and then turned toward her father, her lower lip quivering, her eyes staring over his shoulders.

"Big-time phileo, Daddy."

"Me you more, my daughter."

Then she squared her shoulders, turned toward the chariot road, and walked away from her home.

CHAPTER SIXTEEN

On the Road

Pandy passed through the wrecked agora and by her school. Now that it was ruined, it looked a lot better. They should keep it that way, she thought. She looked up at the Acropolis, and the still smoldering Parthenon, and the Library, all quiet in the early morning. There was her preschool, Medea's Mini Muse and Happy Hero Day Care. After her first day there she'd begged not to be sent back; she smiled, remembering that none of the other children would play with her because of her connection with fire, squealing that she'd turn them into human toast.

She knew every inch of Athens, every alley, temple, statue, fresh-water tap, and fast-falafel shop. She'd used every back entrance to every market stall. She knew hidden corners where the government officials whispered, the benches where the best philosophers discussed the mysteries of life, and even the secret place the dryads gathered in the evenings. She knew where the message runners went to cool down, the best watering holes for the chariot horses, and which gardens grew the most beautiful flowers.

She'd discovered so many hidden treasures of her beloved city. And she knew that just maybe she'd been taking it all a little for granted, knowing now that she might never see any of it again.

Six hours later, after passing olive groves and grape vineyards, Pandy crested a large hill and turned for a final look at Athens. Her legs ached and her feet were beginning to blister. Sitting down on a patch of grass by the roadside, she determined she had at least two weeks of walking ahead of her, maybe more. She was hungry but felt she had to save her meager stores, although she knew full well she couldn't make her supplies last long. She also knew she should keep moving, but the grass was so soft and it was just nice to look back and see the chariots and runners and oxcarts and people milling about off in the distance . . .

. . . and a snow white dog running toward her ahead of two girls, one of whom kept veering off to the right.

Pandy blinked. She stood up, slightly turning her ankle on a rock and popping a blister.

She watched as the trio got closer and closer. It was taking a while because one girl had to keep chasing the other, who was swerving, and drag her back onto the road. At that point the girl who was being dragged would stomp her feet and swing her arms wildly.

Pandy started to laugh as Dido came racing up the hill, almost knocking her down. She heard Iole's and Alcie's voices coming over the last fifty meters.

"I still think we should put you on a leash, Alcie! It might help," said Iole.

"I don't *need* any . . . unh!" Alcie cried, crashing into a laurel tree.

Dido was sniffing at the leather pouch.

"Stop it . . . not for you!" said Pandy.

"Apricot right, it's not for him!" panted Alcie, coming up the hill. She was taking it on an angle, trying to walk toward Pandy as straight as possible. "He's been after our food and water all day. I've been yelling my head off."

"Shrieking like a siren," said Iole, joining them.

Pandy started to cry again.

"You guys . . . what are you doing . . . you can't . . ."

"Don't gimme any of that, you ungrateful little grape!" Alcie cried, slapping her hand over her mouth. Then she parted her fingers to be able to speak. "Sorry. Look, we've been up all night, stealing food from the cupboards, getting blankets; Iole even found her new 'You're a Maiden Now!' sandals and she wasn't supposed to get them for another three moons, so don't try to telling us to go back, because we won't."

"Pandy, we *discoursed* about it all day after you left . . . ," Iole said.

"She means we talked about it," said Alcie.

"Right," said Iole. "The school is in shambles so it's out at least until the end of the planting season. Nothing is healing my bumps. Maybe somewhere out there we'll find a cure for them . . . or for Alcie's feet. Look, I brought my dad's old sword!" She pulled a short sword out of her carrying pouch. "The blade's kinda bent, but . . . but . . . We *can't* go back, Pandy. Unless we help you save the world, there won't be much to go back to. Anyway, you need us. We're not all best friends for nothing, you know. And if you think for a minute we'd let you go off alone and get killed or worse when we could be right there getting killed or worse with you . . . then you just don't know us at all!"

"Lemon right!" said Alcie. "I think."

"Okay, now look, I'm totally serious about this," said Pandy. "You guys . . . I love you both so much, but you have to go back. If Zeus finds out . . ."

"Wrong-o!" said Alcie.

"Pandy, if the whole thing happened just the way you say it did," said Iole calmly, "then Zeus only said that no one in your *family* could help. Well, we're not family . . . not really . . . so no one gets boiled in oil. He can't go back on his word. Can he, Alcie?"

"Who gives a fig," Alcie answered. "I'm just glad to be out of my house!"

Pandy held back her tears and buried her face in Dido's fur.

"How did you get him to follow you?" she asked.

"Follow *us*?" yelled Alcie. "That flea-farm was lying outside your courtyard wall when I passed by on my way to Iole's. He spotted me on the ridge and ran up all excited. It's like he knew what we were doing. He basically dragged me over to Iole's. And then when we were leaving, he took off like a crazed marathon runner. We've been trying everything we know to keep up with him. He doesn't seem to care about *my* little problem!"

Alcie glared down at Dido, who conveniently looked away.

"I think he didn't want you to get too far, Pandy," said Iole, with a giggle.

"But your parents . . ."

". . . will be worried sick, blah, blah, blah," said Alcie.

"We know," answered Iole. "It just can't be helped. This is too important."

"We can at least get word to them that you're okay," said Pandy.

"How in Hades can you do that?" asked Alcie.

"You'll see . . . not just yet," she said, looking at the cloudless sky overhead. "It's amazing. At least that's what Dad says."

"Right. I'm done panting," said Iole. "Let's go."

Pandy's smile began to stretch clear across her face. The girls linked arms with Alcie in the middle so they could steer her straight. Pandy felt as if her backbone were made of adamant as the four of them turned three backs and one tail on the city of Athens and walked on up the road.

They had several uneventful days of walking past farms and laurel groves, and fording small streams. They used Iole's bent sword to hack their way back through overgrown thickets whenever Alcie strayed too far off the main road.

"May rocks fall on your heads!" she'd cry. "It doesn't help that I have a right sandal on a left foot, you know!"

They knew that three young maidens and a dog alone would attract some attention, so they skirted around the larger cities like Thebes and Eleusis. At smaller towns or villages they came to, however, they'd ask directions to Delphi. The first time, Pandy went into a tavern alone and mistakenly approached a petty thief who, seeing her splendid silver girdle, decided to relieve her of it. Pandy managed to run out before he could snatch it. The thief followed, only to find Dido, teeth bared viciously, waiting for him outside. That was the last time any of them went anywhere alone.

Their nights were mostly quiet, in an eerie, apprehensive way. The very first night Pandy pulled out the map and showed them its strange symbols and the ring with the single number 179 on it. Then, as soon as she felt it was safe, Pandy took the conch and spoke into it softly. Then she held it to her ear and only had to wait an instant before she heard her father's voice on the other end. Iole gasped and Alcie leaned in closer to hear Prometheus. Pandy told her father everything: that the girls and Dido were with her and that everyone was safe. After holding the shell away from her ear so they could hear him screaming, Pandy convinced her father not to come charging after them, but only to get word to their families that both girls were all right.

Pandy introduced Alcie and Iole to her diary and told of their day's travels each night as the girls rested. The wolfskin relayed information from Dido about nearby fresh water, or what creatures were watching from the bushes and what protections they should take. They shared two blankets and Sybilline's cloak, staying warm with Dido sleeping on their feet; although occasionally Pandy would feel Iole's bumps wiggle as they snuggled and sometimes Iole would wake with a giggle in the middle of the night. Once it rained, forcing them all to find shelter underneath a small cluster of myrtle tress. As Alcie and Iole spread the blankets on the ground, Pandy casually gathered a little pile of twigs. When the others weren't looking, she blew gently and soon had a glowing pile giving off lots of heat. Alcie and Iole were startled, but Pandy held up two twigs.

"I just rubbed them together." She smiled.

"Oh . . . well, sure. I coulda done that, too," said Alcie.

Pandy spoke briefly with her father at night, always ending her conversation with "Big-time phileo, Dad." Alcie and Iole began to playfully mimic "Me you more, my daughter" as Prometheus said it on the other end. Then the three best friends would curl up like spoons, exhausted, and doze off.

However, on the third night out, they were all intermittently awakened by a peacock screeching somewhere close by.

"Idiot pea-kook!" grumbled Alcie the next morning, trudging a winding stretch of road, all of them bleary eyed from lack of sleep.

"Well, it's Hera's bird . . . ," Pandy said, "and she gave me the map . . . maybe it's a signpost of some sort."

"Maybe it's telling us that we're on track," said Iole, sounding hopeful.

From the tension in her stomach, however, Pandy knew Iole was wrong, just as she'd known on Olympus that Hera's intentions were not what they seemed. But she wasn't about to tell this to Alcie and Iole.

"Maybe it doesn't have to be so *loud* when it tells us," said Alcie. "Apples! I'd like to wring its scrawny neck."

"Alcie, keep your voice down," cautioned Iole.

"Whatever!"

On the morning of their eleventh day, they crested a high hill that looked down on a beautiful valley. The great city walls of Delphi were visible on the side of Mount Parnassus, as it rose majestically in the distance. Iole figured they were within five kilometers of the city.

"We'll be there for mid-meal," she said, descending into the valley.

"Goody, more dried fruit!" scoffed Alcie. "Dee-li-cious!"

A little while later, they were coming around a curve and Alcie was trying out a new step, walking sideways and crossing one leg over the other (which, in addition to slowing them all down, was absolutely not working), when Dido stopped short, every muscle in his body taut like the string on a bow. He was staring at something far up the road. Pandy squinted, but she could see nothing.

"What's up there, ghost dog? Huh?"

Dido was both growling and whimpering, almost as if he were afraid and eager at the same time.

"Look. There's . . . something," said Iole, squinting into the distance.

Pandy saw two shapes emerge from some large bushes into the main road. Dido took off running, got about twenty meters, turned around in a circle several times, and barked back at the girls. Then he ran another few meters and barked again.

"Don't know if you know this," said Alcie, "but your dog's a freak."

"Come on," said Pandy, hurrying after Dido.

"That freak·is finding water and keeping you from going thirsty, Alcie," said Iole.

"Oranges! Let's go."

Ten meters from the two figures, Dido stopped abruptly and went rigid again, but the girls saw that these two were nothing more than an incredibly old woman leading a goat on a loose cord. The woman seemed frightened of Dido, but the goat was staring the dog down. Pandy noticed that the sky had suddenly become dark and overcast, and it was getting darker every second.

"I'm sorry about my dog. He's usually very friendly," said Pandy, grabbing Dido's scruff.

"Perhaps he sees my poor old goat as a tasty little treat, hmm?" said the old woman, her voice sounding like two sheets of papyrus rubbed together. Strands of thin white hair fell around her crinkled face and trailed down her back, over her filthy and tattered brown robes, to the ground.

"Gods!" said Alcie loudly to Iole. "She's even older than Sabina!"

The old woman casually turned her filmy eyes toward Alcie.

"Shh," said Pandy, then turning to the woman, "Please forgive my friend . . . she's been sick, and we're all very tired."

"Of course," said the old woman. "We're hunting for berries or roots, anything to feed little Laodon and myself."

"Laodon? That's a wonderful name!" said Iole, petting the goat behind its ears. "Are you hungry? Huh?"

"Perhaps you have something to share with us . . . just a morsel of flatbread. A dried grape? A slightly gnawed olive pit?" said the woman.

"Hades, no!" said Alcie. "We barely have enough for ourselves! As if!"

Pandy grabbed Alcie's arm and pinched her hard.

"Ow!" Alcie squealed.

"Excuse us for just a second," said Pandy to the woman as she and Iole dragged Alcie off to the side of the road.

"Alcie! You're being uncouth," said Iole.

"I am not . . . whatever that means. I'm being smart!"

"We're going to have to get more food anyway," said Pandy.

"We're going to starve before we get to Delphi, you flesh-eating Charybdis!" said Alcie. "Am I the only one here doing any thinking?"

"I'll give them some food, Pandy," said Iole.

"So will I. And so will *you*," Pandy said, glaring at Alcie.

Pandy walked up to the old woman, now talking quietly to her goat.

"I'm so sorry," said Pandy, "but it's true. We're on kind of a long journey, but of course you can have something."

She started rooting in her pouch for her food sack.

"Iole, open your sack. Alcie, you too!" Pandy said.

She looked up to offer what she could to the old woman and gasped. Iole looked up and dropped her sack in terror. Alcie simply fainted.

The two pathetic creatures were gone. In their place stood Athena, an enormous owl perched on her wrist, and Hephaestus, sooty and misshapen, but still strikingly impressive. Pandy knew them at once, but Iole was shaking with fear.

"Do not be alarmed, little one," said Athena to Iole, then she clucked to her owl. "Tyro, go!"

Pandy kept Iole steady as Athena quickly lifted her arm and the owl went soaring overhead. They watched as Tyro circled again and again in a slow descent. Spreading out like a streamer behind him was a fine golden thread, which settled, concentrically, on a large clump of nearby bushes. There seemed to be no change to the bushes whatsoever, but Athena motioned everyone over to a small opening between two shrubs as Tyro landed on her arm. Hephaestus delicately picked up Alcie as if she were a feather and carried her in his arms.

They found themselves in a lavishly decorated tent, exactly the same mottled yellowish greenish color as the foliage, but quite spacious inside. At their feet were intricately woven rugs; each designed to blend in with the colors of the ground. Athena beckoned them to plop down on velvety-soft cushions in rich browns and rusts. Small tables were laden with plates of steaming fresh foods and goblets of juice. Dido immediately wolfed down a dog bowl of roasted lamb and then settled on his back on top of a beautiful rug, rolling around with delight. Pandy and Iole each started to reach for a goblet, but were startled into stillness by Athena's voice.

"We are here but a moment, Pandora. We shall be brief and you must listen carefully. Hephaestus?"

Alcie, lying on a muted yellow cushion, was starting to come around.

"This is for you, daughter of Prometheus," said Hephaestus, stepping forward on his spindly legs. From a silk pouch at his waist, he withdrew the gold and adamantine net and handed it to Pandy. "We know what you seek. This will ensnare whatever you desire; use it well and wisely."

"Very good," Athena began. "And now I give you . . ."

"Do I need to be more specific?" He turned to Athena, whispering. "I mean, it's very straightforward, but then again I made the thing. Maybe I need to demonstrate, huh? That's it, I'll demonstrate . . ."

"No," said Athena, rolling her eyes. "She gets it. You get it, right, Pandora?"

"Yes, I do! I do! Oh, thank you, wonderful Hephaestus!" Pandy put the net in her pouch, then impulsively dashed forward to kiss his cheek.

"Oh! Oh! I'm so very, very sorry!" Pandy said, bowing low, mortified.

But Hephaestus, smiling, put a huge hand to his face and blushed seven different shades of pink. He looked at Iole and winked.

"Gaa . . . ack . . . ," Iole stammered.

Alcie was now on her feet, not having the vaguest idea where she was, eyes large as serving platters.

"Ah, decided to awaken, have you? The one who doesn't believe in sharing," said Athena sharply.

Alcie opened her mouth to answer, but Pandy wasn't taking any chances. Leaping up, she covered Alcie's face so quickly that Alcie had no time to make a sound.

"It's my fault, great Athena. She was standing close to the box when everything flew out and she's . . . she's . . . not like this all the time!"

But Athena was now staring directly into Alcie's eyes.

"I don't care if the breath is leaving your body, Alcestis Artemisia Medusa. When someone less fortunate than you is in need or want, do what you can, do what you must. You are of noble birth so start acting like it, box or no box! Take a lesson from Pandora. You never know when you might be talking to someone who may aid you during this difficult journey . . . like a god!"

Athena turned away, but added, "I might have fixed your feet, you know, if you'd been at all nice. Not now, of course, but maybe later . . . we'll see. Don't want to do too much at one time. Don't want to prick up any ears back home. Now, Pandora, I'm giving you a little something. It's not a big deal like the net, but it might come in handy."

She pulled out of the air a small marble bust of herself about the size of an orange.

"I cannot travel with you," she continued, "but this will speak words of wisdom on my behalf. If you are troubled or in doubt, ask this bust and it will answer. However, it will give the answer only once and the tongue may get stuck a little. Design problems, I'm sorry to say. Marble is tough. Try not to use it too often. And only at night, if you can, or when it's cloudy."

Pandy took her hand away from Alcie's mouth and pinched her arm to indicate that Alcie should remain silent as she accepted the bust.

"Thank you, mighty Athena. Thank you both! You have no idea how much—"

"Oh don't be silly, of course we do," said Athena. "All right then, we must be gone quickly. Oh, by the way, I've filled your food sacks with some fresh provisions and added unlimited flatbread and dried fruit. It's not lamb, but you kids won't starve. Hephaestus?"

"Um . . . on to Delphi!" was all he could think of to say before Athena waved her hand. Then they and the camouflaged tent with all its contents disappeared, and the sky was once again a cloudless blue.

Pandy opened her leather pouch to put the bust inside, thinking that she would have to smash everything else way, way down to make enough room. But surprisingly, the inside of the pouch, even with everything in it, was very roomy, almost as if it were empty. And the outside of the pouch was flat, not bulging with the mass of sacks and sandals and supplies. She could reach inside and touch everything, yet it seemed bottomless.

"Hey, look what I found!" said Iole.

She held up the thin rope Athena, as the old woman, had used to lead the goat.

"This might come in handy, you never know," she said.

Iole started to wrap it into a loop. She wrapped it several times but the rope, trailing off into the bushes, seemed endless.

"Sirens of Tartarus! It wasn't that long before," said Alcie.

Iole, still pulling and wrapping the rope in loops, looked back at the bushes.

"I think I'm just gonna forget it," she finally said to Pandy. "We can't carry something this big . . ."

Suddenly the other end was in her hand and the coil of rope was complete.

"Huh?" Iole said, startled.

"Lemme see that," said Pandy.

Iole handed her the small coil.

"There's no way . . . we all saw it, right?" said Pandy. "And now it's . . . Well, I guess we don't need something this small. Maybe if it were a little bigger, we might be able to make use . . ."

No sooner had she spoken the words than the coil in her hands added several more loops and the rope itself became a little thicker. Pandy thought hard for a moment.

"Smaller," she said.

The rope shrunk in diameter and lost several loops in length.

"Smaller still," she added.

Instantly she was holding a tiny coil of hemp string.

"It's great!" said Alcie.

"It's brilliant!" said Iole.

"It's going in the bag!" Pandy said, opening her bottomless pouch again. She looked skyward.

"Thank you, Hephaestus. Thank you, Athena."

Dido gave a short bark to get them moving. The sun was almost directly overhead and Iole calculated that they had about four hours of walking to get to the city gates.

"*POMEGRANATES!* I didn't get anything to eat! And that cushion was the softest thing I've felt in days," moaned Alcie.

With Alcie in the middle and Dido in the lead, happy and full of his breakfast, the three girls trudged the last few kilometers to Delphi, with Pandy and Iole taking turns popping dried figs into Alcie's mouth. Just to keep her quiet.

CHAPTER SEVENTEEN

Delphi

They were overwhelmed from the moment they entered through the tall city gates. Delphi, while smaller in area than Athens, had at least twice as many people crowding its streets. Pandy tried to keep hold of Dido's scruff, but finally gave up when the pushing and bumping became too much. Everyone seemed to be moving toward the city center, and the girls were swept along by a river of unbathed limbs and dirty togas. A wide array of scents hit them all at once; they walked in and out of pockets of incense, body odor, patchouli, old wine, garbage, heavy perfumes, soap, and spiced roasting smoke. The city seemed to be one giant marketplace. Everywhere vendors were selling all manner of goods for the weary traveler, tourist, or information seeker, all with one thing in common: they had something to do with the Oracle of Apollo.

There were small replicas of the famous temple on a

hemp string alongside petrified pieces of sacrificial goat. A perfume vendor sold vials of oil, guaranteeing it was the same used at the great altar. There were soaps, lotions, and body salves containing ashes from the sacrificial fires. Papyrus leaflets told of the high priestess's miracle diet; how she'd lost an amazing amount of weight in only two moons: "Learn Her Special 'Sun' Secret!" Leaflets told of oracle phenomena:

"Ithaca man speaks to high priestess, discovers he's dead!"

"Lycian woman's future told: she'll find true love with oxcart!"

For three drachmas, one could buy a small square of flatbread with the image of Apollo and a certificate of authenticity that the Sun-God had touched the bread himself. Or for ten drachmas, four slaves would hoist someone onto a shabby litter and carry her once around a section of the city "in a style befitting the high priestess!"

The girls were shoved and jostled by peddlers, storytellers, magicians, and women selling things that Iole immediately pronounced as "repugnant." There were palm readers, jugglers, wine merchants, and dozens of taverns. Approaching the city center, they were enticed by fake soothsayers who claimed:

"Oracle accuracy 100 percent guaranteed or your drachmas back!"

"Fortunes! Get your fortunes read here, ladies!"

"Everyone's a winner in the tent of Eos the Magnificent!"

"Warts? Leprosy? Lazy eye? Apollo tells *me* what to tell *you* to fix it!"

". . . I'll also guess your weight and your birthday!"

Finally the girls saw ahead of them, across a large open square, the enormous temple that housed the oracle. It was also the home of the high priestess and the acolytes: young maidens training to become priestesses. The temple was at least seventy meters high with immense polished marble columns. Huge oil lamps, their flames continually burning, guarded the entrance. Thousands of people waited to get in, many wringing their hands and weeping. Some were carrying sick children or helping elderly relatives, others were lame or blind or diseased. There were also those who appeared to be physically fine, just interested in what their future held; but these, too, carried an air of tension. How long had these people been waiting, Pandy wondered?

Then she saw the sign on the great temple doors.

"Gone for mid-meal. Back at two."

"Blackberries! I never knew so many people had so many problems!" said Alcie.

"Half of them probably didn't about a month ago," said Pandy. "Come on, let's find someplace where I can think for a moment."

With Dido at their heels, they crossed the square to the nearest tavern and took a small table outside.

"I just realized," said Pandy, "that I have no idea where to look for Jealousy in its purest form. I don't even think I'd know it if I saw it."

"Look into my eyes," said Alcie. "It's the only thing I'm feeling when I see anyone walking normally. Maybe you can get it from me!"

"What will it be, maidens?" asked a stout serving maid, approaching their table.

"Oh, um . . . A goblet of grape juice, please," said Pandy.

"I'd like one as well, thank you," said Iole.

"Wine for me!" said Alcie, folding her arms.

The serving maid, Pandy, and Iole just stared at Alcie. Underneath the table, Dido covered his eyes with his paws.

"What?" Alcie said, glaring back. "Oh, fine . . . grape juice, my good woman!"

"Hey!" Pandy said, as the serving maid walked away. "I'll try asking the bust!"

"Good idea," Iole replied. "You can do it right here."

"Are you kidding? Someone is sure to notice," said Pandy.

Then she looked around the tavern; it was overflowing with unfortunates. People sitting alone, mumbling softly, and glancing at the line to see if it was moving.

179

Couples quarreling. Families trying to keep their children in order, arguing with the serving maid over the size of the bill. One man kept nervously looking at the sky. Another woman just sat at her table and cried. Looking out into the Temple Square, Pandy saw that most people were in some state of desperation and probably wouldn't pay any attention to three girls talking to a statue.

"Well, it's not cloudy or dark . . . but we have no choice," Pandy said.

She casually set her pouch on the table and lifted the flap.

The girls bent forward. To the interested passerby, it looked like they were eating out of a feed bag. Fortunately, no one was interested.

"Great Athena . . . ," she whispered into the pouch.

"Wait!" said Iole. "Pandy, be very careful what you ask it. Remember, it will only answer once."

"I know! I know!" said Pandy. She reached into the bag and brought the bust into the light. "Great Athena, where in Delphi will I find the pure source of Jealousy?"

The eyelids of the little bust flew open. The small irises were the same bright green as Athena's. The tiny mouth was moving awkwardly, as if the tongue were stuck with honey, clicking over some words.

"(Click)-side the temple. Go back to (click). All the way (click)."

The mouth stopped moving as the eyelids closed shut.

"And *thank* you, grrreat Athena!" Alcie groused.

"Shh," said Pandy.

"Well, Alcie's right, Pandy. Is it inside or outside? And why is it telling us to go back? Go back where?" said Iole.

"What time is it?" asked Pandy, putting the bust back into her pouch.

"Twelve thirty," answered Iole, looking at the tavern sundial.

"We have one and a half rotations on the dial until the line starts moving again," said Pandy. "Come on. We'll drink fast. We have no time to waste."

The serving maid brought their goblets of juice, and Pandy and Iole drank theirs down in one gulp. Alcie was taking her time.

"I prefer to sip mine, letting the flavors roll around on my tongue . . ."

"Alcie, if you don't stop . . . ," said Pandy.

"Fine!" she said and quickly drank her juice.

Getting up, they each counted a few precious coins for the bill.

"You've got to leave a gratuity, Alcie!" said Iole.

"Figs to you!" she hissed, but pulled out another half drachma coin.

Pandy led the way back into the Temple Square. By now the line of people waiting was so long, Pandy couldn't see the end.

"Five-headed lizards! That's a lot of people," said Alcie.

"It must stretch back to the city gates," she said. "Let's try this way."

She walked away from the long line and around the far side of the temple. There was much less bustle here, far fewer vendors and street trade: all the real activity was in the front. They passed only a few disinterested tourists, and the girls pretended they were on a school field trip, speaking animatedly about the history of the oracle and what a clayhead their teacher was. Reaching the far corner at the back of the temple, they stopped to get their bearings.

There was a stone wall surrounding the main temple that went up about twelve meters. At the corner, just above them, there was a large decorative statue of a Greek youth, his arm extended back to throw a discus.

"We've got to get up there. There has to be a back way in, right?" asked Pandy.

"Well, in all the temple manuals *I've* ever studied . . . ," said Alcie.

"Quiet, Alcie!" said Iole. "There probably is, especially if there's a terrace up there. The high priestess would need a way of getting out to it without going all the way around the front."

"We can't climb . . . this wall is too high and smooth," said Alcie.

"Ooh, I'm so smart!" said Pandy.

"What?" said Iole.

"The *rope!*" Pandy said.

The three girls looked at one another for a beat, then Alcie pinched Pandy on the arm.

"Ow!"

"Yeah, doesn't feel so great, huh?" said Alcie. "But that was for being a genius!"

"I hope this works," said Iole.

"It has to. The gods don't give things that aren't useful," said Pandy, pulling the small string from her pouch. She held it in her hands and, with Iole and Alcie blocking her from view, said quietly, "Longer."

Instantly the few slender coils grew into many and the width of the rope increased. Pandy quickly tried looping it at one end, but her knots were the simple kind she used to tie her sandal laces. When she pulled the knot tight, it relaxed again and the girls knew it would come loose with any weight on it. She could think of nothing else to do except say, "Make a loop and a knot."

The rope looped over, then twisted and wove its way into a knot so complicated that they couldn't tell where it began or ended.

"Now *that's* a knot!" said Alcie.

Pandy was about to throw the rope up as high as she

could, trying to catch the discus thrower's arm or leg. But she stopped all of a sudden and looked about.

The back area of the main temple marketplace was still fairly deserted, but a few of the food vendors had left their stalls and had congregated in a group for a midday chat. Worse still, a few police-citizens had joined them. A little farther away, a tour group from Corsica was drawing quick charcoal sketches of the temple, positioning and repositioning their friends to get the framing of the pictures just right.

"This is too risky. We need to get these people out of here," Pandy said.

She thought a moment, then pulled her wolfskin diary from her pouch.

"Dear Diary . . . ," she said, unfolding it.

"Blessed you are among mortals. Good evening, Pandora. What do you have to tell . . . ?" said the wolf head, blinking its eyes. "Yes, well. It's sort of *bright* for evening, isn't it?"

"Uh . . . nothing to tell just now. I need your help," she said.

"Well . . . I don't know what I can—"

"Please listen! I need you to tell Dido to create a diversion long enough for us to get up over this wall . . . if we can," Pandy said.

"Ah, yes . . . and *then* what is he supposed to do?" said the diary dryly.

"Tell him to keep out of sight. Have him wait for us behind the tavern we went to earlier, but tell him to keep an eye on the front doors of the temple. When he sees me there, it's safe to come out."

"Very good," said the skin.

"Dido! Come here, boy!" called Pandy, and Dido was immediately at her side. She put the wolf head close to his and the three girls tried to talk as casually as possible over the whines and yelps being traded by dog and diary.

"He understands completely," said the diary at last.

Dido looked up at Pandy, who bent down and put her face to his.

"Good boy! Now go!"

Dido licked her face and took off like an arrow. He stopped in front of a roasted meat vendor, stood on his hind legs, barked ferociously, and snatched a slab of beef off the vendor's cart, causing a general uproar. Next he dashed into a silk traders' stall, where he shook the slab from side to side, splattering juice and meaty flecks all over the costly fabrics. Then he headed down a side alley with a growing mob at his heels. Each of the girls said a small prayer for his safety. Pandy thanked the diary and quickly put it back in her pouch. The back area of the temple was now deserted. Pandy threw the rope up as high as she could, but it came nowhere near to catching the statue.

"Let me try!" said Alcie.

She got a little higher, grazing the leg of the statue, but the rope didn't catch.

Pandy took the rope back and said, "Catch . . . and hold!"

She threw it up again and the rope went sailing higher than ever. The loop caught on the foot of the statue and held fast.

"Let's try something really crazy," said Iole, as Pandy started the difficult climb. "Ask it to pull us up."

"Brilliant! 'Rope, pull us up,'" Pandy said, and the rope began lifting her higher into the air. "Grab on!"

Iole and Alcie caught the rope below Pandy.

"Thanks," said Alcie to Iole from below. "I had no idea in Illyria how I was gonna climb up. You're pretty smart for not even being a maiden yet."

"There's no place for my feet!" said Iole.

"There are little bumps of stone in this wall," Pandy said. "Try to find a toehold here and there; it will help steady you."

"Easy for you to say," said Alcie.

They all reached the top of the wall quickly. Scurrying over the ledge, they saw there was indeed a large back terrace and a small entryway close to one corner of the back wall of the temple.

"Smaller," Pandy said to the rope, and soon it was

a string again, which she tucked into her pouch. They quickly crossed the terrace and gave a light tug on the small door. It opened easily and, without thinking of what lay beyond, the girls entered the Temple of Apollo.

CHAPTER EIGHTEEN
The Temple

It was almost pitch black.

Just above them burned a dim torch. Ahead they could discern other torches burning in sconces. Letting their eyes adjust to the darkness, they found themselves at the end of a long, narrow hallway running along the length of one side of the temple. Pandy, Alcie, and Iole looked at one another.

"Well, we're inside and we're all the way back," said Alcie.

"Those *were* the directions from the bust," said Iole, with a loud giggle.

"Shh!" Pandy said.

"Sorry . . . can't help it," Iole replied.

"Okay. You guys wait here," Pandy said, standing straight and trying to be commanding.

"Like we'd really let you go without us," said Alcie.

"As if!" said Iole, stepping forward.

"I say that!" said Alcie.

"Okay, okay . . . we'll all go . . . but let me go first," said Pandy.

"That works for me," said Alcie.

Pandy led the way slowly in the darkness. They came to an opening in the wall to their right with a narrow stairway leading straight up. Two torches burned brightly high over their heads.

"Do we go up?" asked Iole.

"I don't know," said Pandy. "I think it's probably just living quarters up there. Let's keep going."

Farther down, another torch illuminated a smaller corridor leading off into the darkness. They caught the unmistakable whiff of animals.

"It has to be where they keep the animals for the sacrifices," said Pandy.

"Poor little goats and lambs . . . ," lamented Iole. "Alone in the dark. Probably kept in boxes."

They moved toward another torch burning dimly down the hallway. Drawing near, they could see beyond it part of a lit chamber; they felt the air cool with a slight breeze.

"We must be getting close to the main room," said Iole.

Pandy stopped just before the opening. She flattened herself against the wall and peeked around the corner.

"Oh!"

"What? Let me see!" said Alcie, bending down and craning her neck around Pandy's waist.

"Wow."

"I've never seen anything so immense," said Iole, almost on the floor, peering out from behind Alcie's legs.

"I have . . . the great hall on Olympus," said Pandy. "But this is amazing."

They stepped quietly into the chamber of the great altar.

The enormous room was completely deserted. At the far end were the large doors leading to the Temple Square, bright light glimmering in from the sides. Huge columns stretched way up to support the massive marble ceiling. Oil lamps hung from chains that disappeared into the darkness overhead. Richly colored chalk frescoes along the walls depicted scenes of Apollo healing those diseased in body and spirit. Large white marble collection urns were placed at various intervals to receive tributes and donations. Close to the main doors were sets of shelves where suppliants placed their sandals: anyone allowed to approach the altar had to do so barefoot. An aisle led from the main doors straight through the columns to a small circular area in the middle of the room where, Pandy supposed, suppliants would stand before the high priestess. It was separated from the rest of the hall by a low, circular marble wall, past which no one was allowed to pass.

Pandy saw part of an immense structure to her right. Quietly creeping farther into the room, they dashed to hide behind the columns; now when they peeked out they found themselves directly facing the great altar.

Pandy thought she might stop breathing. She'd never before seen anything so frightening. Beyond the small circle, a series of black stone stairs rose out of the ground. They went up about twenty steps to a flat terrace. From where she stood, Pandy made out two thick slabs of black stone lying side by side with a fissure of hot smoke rising from the crack in between. Hanging in the air over the slabs was a long metal chain with a gigantic hook attached to the end. The hook and the chain were coated with the same black substance as she'd seen on Ares' breastplate on Olympus, and Pandy knew that this was definitely not paint. Beyond the flat terrace, thirty more black stairs led up to a smaller platform, upon which was a simple marble chair.

"Listen!" said Iole.

There was a low rumble underneath the stone slabs. It built in intensity for a few minutes, then suddenly a shower of sparks and a geyser of smoke shot from the fissure with such force that it almost displaced the stones. It quickly subsided again.

"This doesn't look like the altars back home. Do you think they actually lower the little animals into . . . ?" said Iole.

"I don't even want to think about what goes on in here," said Pandy.

"Well, I've seen *sufficient* . . . Let's find this Jealousy thing and get out," whispered Alcie.

Abruptly, a tall woman in stately black and gold robes appeared on top of the altar, screaming something at the top of her lungs back over her shoulder, her dark hair whipping from side to side. From behind her came the sound of yelling in return. The woman grasped the back of the marble chair and began sobbing piteously. She pounded the back wall with her fist and walked to the edge of the platform, her face streaked with tears. Suddenly, a small child (Pandy thought it was a boy) appeared and ran crying to cling to the woman's legs. The woman picked up the child and held him close, whispering something softly into his ear. Then another woman, even taller than the first but wearing almost identical robes, joined them on the platform. She too was shouting and waving her arms.

"You dare to bring a child into my temple! A filthy brat who despoils my home, interrupts the sacrifices with his squalling, and desecrates the great altar!"

"I have been ordained, Callisto!" said the first woman. "I serve as you do. You have no authority to berate me about my child. Nor are you permitted to chastise Nera about her baby. We have as much right to be here—"

"Right? You have no right, Ino! You and Nera . . . with your youth and your experiences and your smiling faces and . . . your . . . children! I'll show you!" said the second woman.

She grabbed the child away from the first woman, Ino, with such force that Ino almost toppled off the platform. Then the second woman, Callisto, walked quickly to the side and lifted the child over her head.

"I'll show you how much right you have in *my* temple!" Then she spoke a few quick words in a low voice that Pandy couldn't hear. At once the giant black slabs far below began to slowly part and Pandy saw a glowing light from a fire somewhere deep under the temple.

Ino screamed once. Then she rapidly began to speak in low tones as well, now grabbing for her son. The slabs stopped moving away and began to close together. Callisto raised her voice higher, still holding on to the child, and the slabs reversed direction again, drawing farther apart. The two women, each holding on to the child, were dueling, their incantations growing in ferocity. Ino, with a fantastic surge of energy, finally closed the stones together again.

Callisto tore the crying child completely away from his mother, and held him precariously over the edge.

"Fire or no fire, Ino, this child dies!" she said and prepared to drop the little boy from the great height onto the black stones below.

Pandy was feverish and dizzy watching this horrifying spectacle. She had no idea what she was doing, but she once again felt as she did standing in front of Zeus: she was not in control of her words as they were being torn from her throat.

"Stop!" she cried, stepping out from behind the column.

Alcie and Iole tried desperately to pull her back, but too late; Pandy was already standing in the main aisle. She stared up at the commotion on the platform, which instantly stopped.

Callisto was so shocked at Pandy's presence in the temple that she momentarily forgot what she was doing and just gaped into the dim light.

Ino immediately took the opportunity and seized her child out of Callisto's grasp. She ushered him away, then quickly came to the edge, also looking down at Pandy.

There was a long moment of silence, then finally Callisto found her voice.

"Trespasser!" she screamed. "Unclean! You approach the altar unbidden? You dare look upon the face of the high priestess unmasked? Your eyes will be torn from their sockets!"

"Callisto, wait . . . ," Ino began, but Callisto turned and struck her so hard across the face that Ino fell dazed against the back wall.

"Silence! I have had enough of you!"

Turning back, she threw wide her arms and began a shrill, high-pitched wail interrupted every so often with strange gibberish words. Callisto's body started gyrating wildly, her head rolling from side to side, her hands fluttering high and low like frenzied birds. Pandy understood almost nothing of what she said, but three times she caught the word *summon*.

Alcie and Iole came out from behind their columns and stared slack-jawed at Callisto, whose voice was now building in volume to a siren scream.

"Strike me dead—look!" said Alcie, pointing upward.

High up toward the marble ceiling, a swirling cloud was forming, twisting, and writhing in upon itself. The girls began to make out the shapes of huge wings with black and white feathers, flashes of silver scales, and long snakelike tails.

Four large flying creatures, winged lizards with hooked beaks and claws, were forming slowly, biting and tearing at one another within the cloud. As the cloud melted away they began swooping down about and around the temple columns; clumsily at first, almost as if they had been formed blind and were just beginning to use their sight. Sweeping past the girls in their flight with growing accuracy, they left behind them a sickening, loathsome stench. Pandy thought of raw meat, eggs, and goat cheese having been left to stew in the sun. Pandy, Alcie, and Iole began to run from column to column trying to find some escape, but they each doubled over from the disgusting odor, feeling nauseous and light-headed.

"Oh, no! I . . . I know what they are!" yelled Iole, as she fell against a column. "Harpies! The hounds of Zeus! Oh, Gods! Pandy, they're Harpies!"

From the platform, Callisto gestured wildly to the three girls and screamed at the flying Harpies, now dive-bombing Pandy, Alcie, and Iole with pinpoint precision. The girls' only protections were the large width of the columns and their ability to skirt quickly from side to side. But Alcie either kept crashing into columns as she tried to get around or veering out into the main aisle, leaving herself exposed. A Harpy spotted her from above and dove toward her. Alcie saw it coming and tried to duck quickly behind a column, but smashed her shoulder into the marble instead.

Pandy had run to a front corner of the temple, trying to move in the dim shadows around the side walls. She was intent on getting to Iole, who had managed to crawl to the large front doors and was trying in vain to dislodge the wooden bolt that ran across, but it was simply too heavy. Pandy was just about to reach Iole, who was still pushing and pulling the bolt with all her tiny might, when they both heard Alcie smash into the column with a loud crack.

Alcie screamed. Pandy and Iole turned to see the

Harpy's metallic tail whip into Alcie's head and throw her to the ground, where she lay without so much as a twitch.

Iole shrieked and started to crawl toward Alcie. Pandy yelled at her to get back but it was too late. A Harpy, flying the length of the main aisle, its neck craning back and forth, saw Iole on her hands and knees trying desperately to reach her friend. In a swift descent, the Harpy let out a terrifying screech and opened its giant claws. Iole looked up just in time to see the glint of the temple lamps off of a series of metal scales, then two talons locked themselves around her waist and lifted her off the ground.

Pandy was still on her feet, Alcie was lying slumped against a pillar, and Iole was now being carried, unconscious, toward the altar. Pandy raced down the aisle, grabbed Alcie, and quickly dragged her back behind the nearest column. Quickly but gently, Pandy curled Alcie inward around its base. She stepped back out into the main aisle and came face-to-face with a Harpy flying low to the ground.

The Harpy snapped at Pandy's head, catching a small hunk of her hair in its beak. It began to ascend, pulling her head up with it. As she jerked her head away, trying to free herself, the blunt edge of its enormous wing caught her square in the face and almost flipped her on her back. She began to lose consciousness, the vile stench of the

Harpy like a poison surrounding her, only vaguely aware of the burning sensation on her scalp and a feeling of warm wetness trickling down her cheek. She fell backward against the column where Alcie lay.

Pandy's last image was of Iole being flown across the altar and her own nose coming to rest against the top of Alcie's foot.

CHAPTER NINETEEN

Lambs

Pandy awoke, smoke searing her nostrils and a loud noise in her ears. Instantly she recognized the particular burnt smell of special herbs: someone was preparing a sacrificial fire. She tried to move her arms, but they were tied tightly behind her back. She blinked, struggling hard to concentrate on the commotion all around. She and Alcie were both facing the great altar, seated on small wooden chairs in the middle of the supplicant circle, their hands and legs bound fast with thick ropes. Their carrying pouches, cloaks, and supplies were piled in a heap next to them. Beyond Alcie, Pandy caught sight of two temple acolytes in hooded white robes standing next to a large wheel with a coiled chain running up toward the ceiling. At the base of the altar stairs, sacrificial herbs were smoldering in sconces, sending up thick streams of inky smoke. The loud noise she'd heard was Alcie yelling, her eyes wide and focused on a point high above them. Groggily, Pandy followed Alcie's gaze—and her heart stopped.

Iole was hanging above the two stone slabs on the great altar, the large metal hook passed through her little girdle. Her hands and feet were bound, but fortunately she was still out cold. High on the second platform, Ino had been tied to the marble chair and her mouth was gagged. Callisto was standing close to the edge, her face now hidden behind a black silk veil. When she saw Pandy awaken, she began to descend the long stairway to the first platform.

"Pandy, do something! *Figs!* Tell them, Pandy . . . tell them why we're here!" Alcie cried, breaking into wrenching sobs.

Staring at Pandy, Callisto reached the temple floor. She circled the small stone wall and came up behind Pandy.

"You dare to defile the Temple of Apollo? Did you think you would go undiscovered?" she said, moving past Pandy. "Did you think you were clever, sneaking into the hall like a thief? Perhaps you are a thief. What have you come to steal, thief; you and your friends?"

"We're not here to steal anything, you big, fat, decomposing hydra!" shouted Alcie.

"Alcie, shut up!" said Pandy.

Callisto was standing directly in front of Pandy, but when Alcie called her a nine-headed water snake, Callisto moved quickly, her hand outstretched to strike. Her veil fluttered off her face for a second and Pandy saw the long straight nose and high cheekbones of a beautiful older woman, except that now her mouth was pulled back in a contorted grin.

"Wait, O high priestess!" Pandy shouted, stopping Callisto's attack. "It's me! I'm the one . . . I'm the only one who should be here. My friends have nothing to do with why . . . um . . . Please . . . I'll tell you. I come on command from the great Zeu—"

"Should be here? You *should* be here, defiler? I am the only one who *should* be here," spat Callisto, looking up at Ino. "I am surrounded by those who think they are better than me . . . those who think they know more . . ."

Callisto's voice trailed off for a moment, then she turned again toward Pandy.

"I'm amused. You're far too young to be allowed to seek information from the oracle on your own. I see no elders with you, and you obviously entered from the back terrace . . . therefore I can only assume you are all thieves."

Her brown eyes narrowed into razor-thin lines.

"Now I will show you what I do to thieves!"

She walked around the wall and up the first set of stairs.

"I come on command of the great Zeus! I am here for

the plague! You have to listen to me! I have to get Jealousy back!" shouted Pandy.

"A thief and a liar!" Callisto whirled about. "As if the Sky-Lord would allow a sniveling she-worm to do his bidding!"

Callisto was now racing to the second platform, taking two stairs at a time. The low rumble had begun from underneath the slabs as smoke and sparks shot up through the fissure.

"But it's true . . . and I can prove it!" said Pandy.

"May I just say," the high priestess said loudly, reaching the top, "that there are three little lambs that will be very grateful to you and your friends for one extra day of life! Let us now see what I can foretell from the ashes of thieves!"

She began the same strange incantation as before and the stone slabs below began to part little by little. Alcie was now trying so hard to break her bonds that the ropes were cutting into her skin.

"Pandy! Stop her!" she yelled.

The slabs were halfway open when Iole woke up. A blast of smoke and sparks shot out of the glowing pit, but fell short of reaching her. She screamed and thrashed about on the hook.

"Iole, don't move!" Pandy yelled.

The slabs were now almost fully open and Iole stared down into a blazing furnace. With the full intensity of the flames just meters below her, Iole's skin began to redden. The bumps that covered her legs and arms swelled to twice their size.

Callisto finished her incantation and raised her right arm. She brought it down hard against her thigh and the chain started to move downward as the acolytes turned the wheel, slowly lowering Iole into the pit.

"*No!*" Pandy screamed. Never before had she known such panic. Not when the box was opened, not when the floor had disappeared from beneath her on Olympus, not standing before Zeus. Never.

Iole was now only a meter or so from the opening. She was wailing and squirming wildly on the hook. Her bumps, now three times their original size, began to sizzle and pop. Golden liquid sprayed out from each eruption and Pandy saw small, shiny things fall into the flames below. An instant later, beautiful blue-winged creatures the size of small coins flew up out of the pit and into the darkness above.

"THIS IS *SO* NOT GOING TO HAPPEN!" Pandy cried at the top of her voice, straining at the ropes with everything in her.

Suddenly, Pandy went deaf.

She saw everything going on around her but it was all in complete silence. She shook her head, trying to clear her ears. Then she felt a tingling sensation on the soles of her feet. It was more of a burning, actually, and she looked down to see if perhaps a spark had jumped from the pit. But her feet were fine. The fiery sensation spread up her legs, over her torso, and down her arms. The odd thing was, there was absolutely no pain. It was quite comfortable. Then the sensation crept up her neck and enveloped her head. She still saw Iole being lowered another quarter of a meter and Alcie thrashing in her chair. Looking up she saw Callisto smiling at her evil handiwork, mouthing words Pandy couldn't hear. Pandy became aware that her joints were seizing up and her limbs were growing heavy as the sensation of heat permeated her body. The veins above her eyes felt ready to burst.

Then the image of her father unexpectedly filled her head. In her mind's eye, she saw his rough, bearded face bathed in a blue and yellow light.

"We are connected to the eternal flame, Pandora," she heard him say. "Remember, fire is a family friend, part of you . . . part of who you are."

Then, as if by command, Pandy started staring, unwavering, at the opening of the pit and the white-hot glow coming up from underneath. She knew there were no words to utter, only the concentration of her mind to the task.

Silently, she willed the fire to die. No other thoughts existed; she focused only on lowering flames and cooling embers. Using only the force of her mind, she stamped out the furnace below Iole by every means possible. She envisioned throwing water on it, covering it with sand, piling mounds of dirt high into the pit.

Slowly, the fire in the pit began to go out. The flames grew smaller and smaller. Callisto didn't notice at first, her mind occupied with thoughts of how, once the thieves were gone, to best dispose of Ino and Nera. But without the intensity of the heat, she looked down into the pit.

Pandy had managed to quench the inferno, and was concentrating on the residual flames, now barely able to keep themselves going. Callisto screamed and signaled again. The acolytes lowered the chain faster. Iole was almost below the rim of the opening; only a few more meters and she'd be burned by the red-hot ashes. But Iole had stopped squirming and was staring at the diminishing fire below her.

Alcie couldn't see into the pit and had no real way of knowing what was happening. But when she looked at Pandy, she saw her friend sitting straight and still, every muscle in her body bulging as if she were lifting the temple off its foundation. Alcie strained forward to look and saw that Pandy's eyes were completely white. There were no pupils or iris rings . . . nothing but bright, glowing white.

Callisto yelled at the acolytes, who stepped away from the wheel and let Iole's own weight plus the weight of the chain carry her fast into the pit.

"*No!*" Pandy roared as Iole disappeared beneath the rim and into the hole.

Pandy leapt up from her chair, looking at the ropes that, only an instant before, had held her fast. Where they touched her skin, the ropes had been burned away, as if Pandy herself had been made of fire. The heaviness and the fiery sensation were gone, and her hearing had returned. She jumped over the small retaining wall and raced up the stairs. Pandy stopped short of going over the rim herself and peered down into the pit.

Iole, very red but neither blistered nor burned, was staring up at her from where she lay upon a slightly warm mound of sacrificial ash, sniffling softly.

Pandy raised her head up toward Callisto. The high priestess stood gaping for a moment, then, without a word, turned and fled through a small door in back.

"Pandy, I can't get out!" said Iole.

"Oh! Oh, right!" said Pandy. She looked at the acolytes, who stood cowering by the wheel.

"Um . . . raise the chain!" she commanded, and then added, "Please."

The two acolytes instantly obeyed and Iole was lifted out of the sacrificial pit. When she had cleared the rim, Pandy reached out for Iole's hand and swung her over to the flat surface of the platform. After Pandora removed the hook from under Iole's training girdle, the two girls clung to each other, crying in shock.

"Okay . . . *hello*!" said Alcie. "Somebody's still tied to a chair, you twisted little apricots!"

"Oh, Alcie!" said Pandy. She and Iole ran down the stairs and, after a few moments spent undoing some very hard knots, released Alcie from her chair.

Gathering their pouches, Pandy made certain that everything was still inside. With Alcie between them, all three started up the stairs, past the altar pit, and up to the second platform. Ino was still bound to the marble chair, her eyes wide and fearful as she looked at Pandy. As Iole removed Ino's gag, Pandy and Alcie made fast work of her ropes. Ino stood quickly and backed away from Pandy.

"Who are you? Are you god or mortal?"

"Puh-leeze," said Alcie, although there was the slightest tremor in her voice.

"I'm . . . um . . . mortal," said Pandy.

"Well, technically . . . ," Iole began.

"What you did . . . to the fire," said Ino, still staring.

"Yeah. I don't know about that," Pandy replied honestly. "Look, I don't mean to be rude . . . but . . . that woman . . . the high priestess . . . why did she try to kill us? What's going on?"

"Great Apollo . . . my child! Tereus!" Ino interrupted with a start. She dashed from the top platform and through the small door in the back wall.

"Wait!" cried Pandy.

But Ino had disappeared into the darkness.

"Come on," said Pandy, rushing after her with Iole right behind.

"Oh, just wonderful . . . ," said Alcie, hoisting her pouch over her shoulder and following as best she could.

CHAPTER TWENTY
The High Priestess

They were once again in a dim, narrow corridor lit only by torches.

"Maybe we shouldn't go so fast," Iole said, walking through the muted light. "There might be someone waiting for us around a corner . . . or something."

"Good . . . not so fast. I love that idea," whispered Alcie, bumping into the wall to their right.

The girls slowed their pace. They passed a steep flight of stairs leading down to their right.

"Those must be the stairs we went by on our way in," said Alcie.

A few moments later, moving as silently as they could, they saw a soft light at the end of the corridor and heard faint voices.

"Callisto? Callisto, come out." Ino was rapping furiously on a door. "Oh, Nera, where were you?"

"You know where I was, Ino," said another woman.

"I was at the market picking up Althea's medicine, although it was a little difficult because there was a white dog wreaking havoc . . . oh, never mind. What did she *do,* Ino?"

"Nera, if Apollo doesn't strike us all dead and burn this temple to the ground . . . ," said Ino, shock now hitting her with full force. "She tried to murder three little girls who wandered in during lunch! She opened the pit and was going to burn each of them alive. Alive, Nera! They're probably outside now telling everyone. Where's Tereus?"

"He's right here with Althea," said Nera. Pandy heard the giggles of two little children.

"Nera, this one girl . . . you have no idea. She put out the sacred fire! She did it. At least, I think she did it. Callisto, please come out! We want to help! Nera . . . this girl . . . her eyes were glowing. And the fire simply died. Just like that. Nera, put the children in your room and come help me open this door."

Pandy, Alcie, and Iole had reached the end of the corridor. Before them were the living quarters of the high priestess. There was a large main room with three oil lamps suspended from a high ceiling. Off of this room were two corridors, including the one they were in, and several smaller rooms. Ino was leaning against a closed door at the end of the main room. Another woman, slightly shorter than Ino, with bright red hair and a round face, wearing simple cotton under-robes and holding a baby, was ushering little Tereus into a second room. Pandora had expected bare simplicity and perfect order befitting a chaste servant of Apollo, but there were children's toys scattered everywhere. Clothes were drying on a rope strung between the lamps across the middle of the windowless room. A standing iron floor sconce had been overturned and made into a makeshift toy chariot. One entire wall had been finger-painted in bright colors and there were countless jars of food on the drainage counter, with labels like "strained apricots," "mashed boar," and "feta and fig medley." Pandy flashed on her little brother for a distressing split second.

"Ares' teeth, this is a pigsty!" said Alcie.

"Ahh!" yelled Nera, quickly protecting the baby girl in her arms.

"No!" said Ino. "No, Nera, don't worry . . . this is them! I mean these are the girls. And this is the one who . . ."

Ino crossed the room and took Pandy by the shoulders. She stared into Pandy's face for a moment, her eyes focusing on the Harpy bite on Pandy's head. As Ino embraced her, Pandy saw small streaks of gray in her dark hair, but her blue eyes were bright and her delicate features gave no true indication of her age. Ino released Pandy and looked at Iole.

"And *you,*" she said. "Gods, what you've gone through. Are you all right? What would you like? Let me get you some juice . . . or wine? Should they have wine, Nera?"

"I should," said Alcie.

"Stop it," said Pandy, pinching her.

"I'd like some water," said Iole.

"Come, sit down," said Ino.

She led them to a large table, then poured out three goblets of water. In her own room, Nera placed her baby on a high pallet with wooden railings. Then she gave Tereus some colored chalk and a sheet of papyrus and told him to draw something funny. She returned and sat at the table as Ino excused herself and rapped on the door at the far end of the room.

"Callisto! Please open the door! We only want to help. I'm sure we can find a simple solution," she said.

"There's only one solution," came a muffled answer on the other side. "Both of you . . . get out of my temple!"

"Same old song," said Nera under her breath.

"Callisto, we can't do that and you know it," said Ino.

"Then leave me alone!" said Callisto.

Ino sighed, then came and sat at the table next to Nera. The two women were silent, suddenly at a loss for words. Pandy, Alcie, and Iole looked at one another, also not knowing what to say. There were so many questions; no one knew where to start.

Finally, Alcie broke the tension.

"I didn't know acolytes wore the same robes as the

high priestess," she said, pointing to Ino's clothes. Pandy and Iole looked at Alcie like she had just asked Poseidon if he liked fish.

"They don't," said Nera.

"But . . . aren't you acolytes?" said Pandy.

"No, my dear," said Ino. She pointed to herself, Nera, and the door at the end of the room. "We're the high priestess."

"Ino! You can't!" said Nera.

"What are we going to do, Nera, keep them here so they can't tell anyone? Murder them the way she would have done? I'm sick of this. After what they've been through, they deserve an explanation. Enough is enough."

Ino stood and, moving to a shelf above the drainage counter, took down a small clay jar.

"But I think we should get a little explanation too, yes?" she continued, applying a soothing balm to Pandy's bite. "I don't know how you put out the fire, but we can get to that later. First of all . . . who are you?"

"I am Pandora Atheneus Andromaeche Helena, of the House of Prometheus of Athens, and this is Alcie and Iole," she answered, the balm feeling wonderfully cool against her skin.

"Actually, it Alcestis Artemi—," Alcie began.

"Athens! Why are you here in Delphi?" said Nera.

"I never get to finish a sentence," said Alcie quietly.

Pandy told Ino and Nera the story of her quest, trying to be brief and still give all the important details.

"And this is the net and this is the box," she said finally, withdrawing them from her leather pouch and placing them on the table.

"Brave girls, each of you," said Ino after a long pause. "And your father is the famous Prometheus. Well, that explains the fire."

"How, exactly, does that explain the fire?" said Alcie. "I'm *so* not getting this."

"It's all connected, my dear," said Ino. "Pandora, do you know how your father stole fire from Zeus?"

"Yes . . . he carried it," she replied.

"In what?" asked Nera.

"In his hands," Pandy said.

"In his hands, Pandora!" said Ino.

"I thought he meant a box in his hands," Pandy said.

"Nope," said Iole. "Oh, I get it! I think I get it!"

"I don't," said Alcie.

"It's the legend," said Ino. "He lifted a burning branch from the eternal flame and carried it down off Olympus in his bare hands! He had a Titan's power over the flames. And you have it as well. Is this the first time you've experienced a . . . a . . . closeness with fire?"

"Well, no," Pandy answered. "I can kinda do one other thing."

And she told them all about the trick.

"I knew it!" said Alcie. "I *knew* there was something fishy about that fire you started in the rain."

"I'm not surprised at all," said Iole.

"You mean you knew?" Alcie asked.

"I deduced. But I'm smart," she added.

"Wow . . . totally neat," was all Pandy could think of to say.

Ino and Nera smiled at Pandy's innocence.

"Yes. Very neat. And I've a feeling it will get neater," said Ino.

"Um . . . how can there be three high priestesses? Doesn't that go against the rules?" asked Alcie.

Ino and Nera looked at each other.

"Go ahead, Ino. You might as well," said Nera.

"A few weeks ago, terrible things began happening in the city and the outlying areas," Ino began. "Actually, Pandora, now that you've explained what you've done, it all makes a bit more sense. People were fighting in the streets for no reason, even quarreling over the price of figs, for Olympus' sake. Two men killed each other right on the temple steps. People became depressed and irritable, spouses were unfaithful, gossip, envy, and hate were everywhere."

"People started coming to the temple in droves," Nera continued. "The oracle was going constantly. You saw the long line waiting to get in? Well, that is merely a fraction of what we deal with day after day after day. But we're a public service; we have to be there for the populace. Callisto has been the high priestess, we just say THP, of the temple for many, many years; it's a position that's been in her family for generations. But people began leaving the temple unsatisfied—"

"Frightened, actually," Ino broke in.

"Right," Nera agreed. "Many were questioning her words, not really believing they were receiving messages from Apollo. Also, her attitude had changed. She'd become vicious in her prophecies. Especially toward . . ." Nera broke off, looking into the room where her baby was sleeping soundly and Tereus was eating his colored chalk.

". . . children," Ino picked up. "The Council of City Elders received so many complaints from mothers who'd been told to harm or even kill their children as sacrifices to Apollo that they had to take action."

"Why doesn't she like children?" asked Pandy.

"No one knew that she didn't, at first," said Ino.

"We only knew," said Nera, "that she was exhausted and her prophecies were faulty. She told one man he would live only to the age of sixty-five, and he was already seventy-one. The council couldn't simply remove her, for fear of angering Apollo . . ."

"Besides, it's a civil service job . . . *can't fire, must retire*," said Ino.

"But," Nera went on, "no acolytes were ready to assume her position. Also, the city couldn't afford her pension and a new THP. Besides, she's not equipped for anything else: what's a chaste and barren woman with very few skills going to do?"

"Barren?" said Iole.

"Yes," Nera continued. "The high priestess must not only be chaste and avoid the company of men, but it's always helpful, though not entirely necessary, that she be unable to conceive a child as well. Callisto fit the bill perfectly."

"The council just wanted to take a little pressure off her," said Ino. "So we were brought in as part-time THPs. I was working at the oracle on Mount Ossa, which was destroyed when Ossa erupted."

Nera cut in. "And I was oracling in Thebes. Oh, the pillaging and looting! I'm lucky little Althea and I got out alive."

"Didn't you have to be chaste?" asked Pandy.

"Ah . . . yes. That," said Nera. "Well, you see, I'd left the prophecy business about two years ago. I met a man . . . my darling Thersander. He used to service the temple well at Thebes and we got to talking . . . oh, he was the nicest guy. I realized I wanted a little more out of life than soothsaying offered, even with the pension and benefits. So I retired and married. And then I had Althea seven months ago. Thersander was called to war about two months after that. I received word a little later that . . . um . . . he'd been killed."

Nera looked away. She tried to smile, but it was very hard for her to continue.

"When the position opened up," she said after a bit, "I prayed to Apollo, we talked, and he agreed that these were desperate times. So one, two, three . . . and he restored me."

"Huh?" said Alcie.

"Well," said Nera, "you can't work in a temple and not be a virgin. It's the primary qualification to be a priestess. You girls know that."

The three girls lowered their eyes, then, trying to be subtle, each looked up at Ino.

"You're wondering about Tereus, aren't you?" Ino asked.

Pandy shrugged. Iole nodded. Alcie slapped her hand over her mouth.

"My sister and her husband were killed during a Spartan raid over a year ago, leaving my little nephew an orphan. The Temple at Ossa was very gracious and let me officially adopt Tereus as mine. We're a package deal; take me, take him. I've never been restored," Ino said, smiling gently at Nera. "I'm still 'stored.' "

"Anyway, nobody discriminated. It was all very 'don't ask, don't tell, and keep the kids quiet,'" said Nera.

"So," said Ino. "We answered the Delphi Council's ad and after extensive interviews started here. I've got the early evening, late-night shift. Nera has graveyard and Callisto still has nine to five."

"But she went insane when we were brought in," Nera said. "Wouldn't let us work, told us we were usurping her authority. Ridiculed our soothsaying."

"Nera and I can usually handle her," Ino continued, "but we have to keep the children out of sight. Today, she caught Tereus in her room, just crawling around, and she went mad. These quarters are cramped, but we try to make do. The general population doesn't know, though, because we're in the same robes and under veils. The acolytes are sworn to secrecy. And only one of us ventures out during lunch and always in disguise."

"Wow," said Alcie. "That's rough. Job cut way down. Surrounded by kids. I wonder if she ever even wanted any."

"Great Gods!" cried Pandy. "That's it!"

"What?" said Iole.

"It's her!"

"Her who?" said Alcie.

"Don't you all see? She hates children. Why? Because she can't have any! She never had a choice. And now she has to share the only thing she loves, her job, with two women who can do both: serve as THPs *and* raise their babies. It's killing her. She's the source. She *is* Jealousy!"

They heard a sudden, loud crash behind Callisto's door and Ino leapt from the table just as everyone heard Callisto scream.

CHAPTER TWENTY-ONE
Jealousy

"Callisto, are you all right?" Ino called, approaching Callisto's door.

"Stay away!"

"The girls, Callisto?" Ino went on. "The three girls? They're fine. They're right here, absolutely unharmed . . ."

Callisto's door flew open and she stepped into the main room, almost knocking Ino off her feet. Her hair was undone, her robes streaked with spots from her tears, the veil dangling under her chin. She was holding a broken shard from a looking glass that she'd smashed, her finger trickling blood.

"They're in my home?" she raged. "My temple has been desecrated and now you allow vermin into my home? Apollo will strike you all!"

"Vermin? Excuse me, but you tried to kill us. Remember?" said Alcie.

"And I would have succeeded but for an evil sorcery!" she said, beginning to shake violently, tearing at her hair.

Little Althea began crying on her pallet.

"I will kill that child!" screamed Callisto, raising the glass shard and rushing toward Nera's room.

Nera sprang up instantly and rounded the table, preparing to tackle Callisto. Ino darted forward, but Callisto tripped over Alcie's two left feet sticking out from under the table, falling with a heavy thud to the floor. The glass flew out of her hand and shattered in a far corner. Callisto lay gasping for breath, unable to move.

Little Tereus, bored with his chalk and papyrus, appeared from Nera's room and scampered over to Callisto, apparently forgetting that she'd nearly smashed him to bits an hour earlier.

"Hi! Hi!" he giggled, patting her forehead, as Ino pulled him away.

Callisto opened her eyes to look at Tereus. A single tear ran down her cheek. Then she began to convulse. Small spasms at first, but they grew in strength until her entire body was seizing and releasing miserably.

"Oh, no! Not again," said Nera.

"What's happening?" said Pandy.

"Same thing happened yesterday. I didn't have a chance to tell you, Ino," said Nera, moving swiftly to get a drying cloth. Callisto was now thrashing so hard she hit her head on the floor tiles. Then she lay very still, her eyes wide and her mouth open.

"What can we do?" said Pandy.

"Stay back and don't touch it," said Nera.

"Touch what?" said Pandy and Ino together.

"Look!" said Alcie.

From Callisto's mouth, a thick black sludge was oozing slowly across the floor like a flat black worm.

"Pandy . . . !" whispered Iole.

But Pandy could only gape as the oozing sludge finally drained from Callisto's mouth and pooled in a small circle on the floor. Then, as they all stared, the sludge pool thickened and rose up, forming itself into a jagged black rock.

"Great Zeus," said Nera. "That didn't happen before."

"What do you mean?" said Ino, holding Tereus back.

"I mean she just seized up and that black . . . stuff . . . came out. I went to get a cloth to clean it up, but it had disappeared when I returned!" said Nera, wrapping a cloth tightly around her hand, staring at the black rock, which was now vibrating slightly.

"Pandora!" said Iole.

"What?" she said, looking at last at Iole.

Iole looked at the vibrating rock, then back at Pandy. Instantly, Pandy understood.

"Of course!" she cried and lunged across the table for the golden net.

"Ugh!" she heard Alcie say.

"Apollo protect us!" said Ino.

The jagged, vibrating rock, now shot through with ugly green veins, had sprouted six tiny black legs and was crawling deliberately back across the floor toward Callisto's open mouth. Callisto, unable to move but perfectly able to see, began to whimper as the rock came closer.

"Nera, hurry!" yelled Ino.

"Get away from it, Nera," said Pandy loudly. Nera, so startled by Pandy's command, backed away immediately.

Unfolding the net, Pandy pushed past Alcie and Nera. One leg of the rock was now on Callisto's quivering bottom lip and the rock was about to hoist itself into her mouth when Pandy threw the golden net neatly over it, stopping the rock dead. As Callisto fainted, Pandy bent down and swiftly grabbed the rock and the net off the floor, holding the net at arm's length.

"Alcie . . . get the box," she said.

Alcie quickly pulled it from Pandy's pouch.

"Here!"

"Okay," Pandy said. "Alcie, turn the box so that it opens toward me. Iole, stand next to Alcie and be ready to help her shut the lid. Okay . . . okay . . . now, Alcie, I'm going to count to three, then you open the lid . . . but not too wide. Then close it again once this thing is inside. Got it?"

"Duh!" said Alcie, as Iole stepped beside her.

Pandy cupped her hand around the black stone and peeled the rest of the net away for a clear throw. The little rock was vibrating, its tiny legs trying to claw through the adamantine threads. Then one leg found an opening, poked through, and pierced her forefinger.

At once, Pandy was drowning in feelings unlike anything she'd ever known. She was inferior and ugly, only ten times more than anyone else: jealous of everyone for everything and so, so bitter about her life. She wanted things; basically everything she didn't have. She wanted Helen's hair (before she'd been reduced to a salamander) . . . and Iole's brain . . . and her mother's beauty . . . and a boyfriend. She wanted to be anyone else. She wanted, wanted, wanted. Her eyes were closing and her mind was going black, like a starless, moonless night.

"Pandy!" said Iole.

"Shut up . . . ," Pandy mumbled, starting to slump forward.

Iole stepped toward her and grabbed Pandy's shoulders. Using all of her strength, she shook her friend hard—very hard.

"Pandy!"

Pandy's eyes flew open wide.

"Put it in the box!" said Alcie.

Everything was clear again, but Pandy had no idea how long the clarity would last.

"One, two, . . . three!" she cried.

Alcie lifted the lid, Iole's hand hovered just above it. Holding the net, Pandy quickly tossed the black rock inside the box. With a terrible hiss, the rock began to fizzle away into smoke. Immediately Pandy felt the blackness lift from her soul.

"Now!" Pandy said, and Alcie snapped the lid shut, just as a fine silver mist began to rise out. Feeling the smallest twinge of regret that something as wonderful as Hope was now trapped with Jealousy, Pandy took the box, flipped the adamantine clasp down, and, pulling a pin from her hair, slid it through the clasp to hold it fast.

She put the box on the table and backed away. Pandy, Alcie, and Iole all looked at one another. The next instant, they were whooping and jumping with glee.

"We did it!"

"You did it."

"But *you* knew!"

"How did you know?"

"She's smart!"

"Do you think that's it?"

"It's the only thing it could be!"

"I'm smart too, you know!"

"It was easy!"

"Easy? We were almost toasted!"

"Girls! Girls!" said Ino. "Would you pull out a chair while we get Callisto up?"

"Oh, of course," said Pandy. They helped ease Callisto,

now coming out of her faint, into a seat at one end of the table. Pandy put the box and the net back in her carrying pouch and set it far down at the other end.

Callisto's head hung forward loosely and there was a small cut on her lower lip where the rock had tried to crawl back inside.

"Nera, eucalyptus oil, please," said Ino.

Nera quickly delivered a small glass vial of pale yellow liquid. Ino waved it under Callisto's nose and, with a hiccup, Callisto raised her head, looking at everyone around her.

"Callisto? How do you feel?" asked Ino.

Callisto looked at Ino and Nera for a moment, then turned a blank stare on Pandy, Alcie, and Iole.

"I'm fine," she said at last. Her voice was dry and scratchy, but the tone was kind and majestic. "Nera, why are these maidens in our chambers?"

"What do you remember, Callisto?" asked Ino.

"Nothing," she said quietly, after a moment. "Nothing. Why?"

"How about the Harpies, huh? Ow!" said Alcie, as Pandy pinched her.

Silence surrounded the table as, once again, no one knew where to begin. Tereus began wriggling and whining in his mother's arms, almost breaking free. Callisto looked hard at the child for a moment. Then she opened her arms and managed a feeble smile.

"Come here, little one."

Ino let Tereus go and he ran to Callisto. He stopped short and did a funny little dance, teasing her. But Callisto caught him up and set him on her lap.

"Are you going to tell me what's been happening, hmm?" she said, smiling gently at Tereus.

"No!" he shouted playfully.

"I will," said Ino.

"We'll help," said Iole.

An acolyte appeared in the corridor entrance, her head bowed in subservience. She and Nera exchanged a few hushed words.

"Well," she said, turning back. "Apparently we're close to having a riot. The line of supplicants now supposedly stretches all the way back to Thebes. I'll go and prophesy, Callisto, you sit and rest."

As she passed, Callisto reached out and took her hand, bringing Nera up short.

"Thank you, Nera."

"My privilege," Nera replied. "Ino, when Althea wakes up, would you give her the cough medicine?"

"Of course . . . see well!" said Ino.

Nera donned the veil and robes of the high priestess and walked swiftly down the corridor toward the altar.

Over the next hour, Pandy related her story to Callisto, with Ino and Iole adding necessary information and Alcie adding a few unnecessary comments. Callisto sat hushed, focusing on the time and day that the box was first opened. When Ino began to blend in the events happening since she and Nera arrived at the temple, however, Callisto's lower lip quivered and tears fell from her eyes. And when Ino and Pandy told of the Harpies and the near murder of Iole, Callisto hung her head and gave in to silent wracking sobs. Everyone at the table felt completely helpless. Finally, Callisto raised her head.

"The Harpies are only to be called when the temple is truly threatened. It was an oath I swore to Zeus," she said, then looked at Iole. "Dear Iole . . . I don't know how I can do anything that you will accept as an apology, but let me try. You know, I have a wonderful healing salve for your bumps . . . where are your bumps? Aren't you the one with the bumps?"

Pandy and Alcie gasped.

Iole's bumps were gone. Her skin was almost perfect; only the faintest circles indicated where the bumps had been.

"Well, I guess I just needed to be hung over a sacrificial fire and almost roasted to death. Who knew?" she said.

With that, everyone smiled the first real smiles they had known in days.

"I remember almost nothing of the last few weeks," Callisto said at length. "But if I am correct, then at the time the box was opened, I was prophesying for a young mother whose child had been born blind, and Apollo was clearly giving me a message of healing and encouragement for her. But as I began to relay this, something . . . an insect, I thought . . . flew into my mouth. I felt a sharp, twisting pain in my abdomen as if I had swallowed glass. I can recall very little after that, except that the woman ran from the temple crying. I didn't know why and I didn't care. I felt emptiness consuming me. I was sensitive only to my own bitterness, not knowing how miserable I was making those around me."

Pandy thought about how horrible she'd felt only minutes before and couldn't imagine living with those feelings for weeks.

"In the last few days," Callisto said, "I became aware that whatever was inside me was going to kill me if I didn't rid myself of it. I knew I'd been having seizures, and I'd watch that thing crawl in and out. Today I smashed my looking glass; I was going to cut it out of me."

She looked stricken, not only at how she'd behaved, but also at what might have happened.

"I am profoundly sorry," she said, trembling.

"It's not your fault, Callisto," said Ino.

"You can't help it if you were born barren," said Alcie.

Her hand flew instantly to cover her mouth.

"I'm sorry. Oranges! Stop pinching me!" she said, rubbing the welt that Pandy had just given her.

"Then stop being dumb!"

"I said I was sorry."

"It's all right, both of you," said Callisto. "You're right, Alcestis, it's not my fault, really. The Fates did not decree that I should have children, only that I should deeply want and love them. A blessing and a curse. I have been especially able to intercede with the great Apollo on behalf of children, but my desire has always been kept in check and served me well, until now. It is also what made me so vulnerable."

"Actually, it's kind of a neat situation," said Pandy.

"What is, Pandora?" said Callisto.

"Well, if Nera and Ino are part-time THPs, then whoever isn't working or sleeping gets to take care of the children. It just makes sense. Callisto, you can be a part-time mother."

After a full ten seconds, Callisto's jaw hit the table.

"We won't always be here, Callisto," said Ino tenderly. "When Pandy gets everything back into the box and things settle down, the council won't need us anymore, but until then . . ."

"Would you let me, Ino? You and Nera?"

Just at that moment, Althea woke on her pallet, coughing uncontrollably.

Ino instinctively rose from the table, stopped short, then sat right back down again and looked at Callisto.

"Althea's medicine is on the small table by her pallet.

Just two drops under her tongue, but then you have to hold her until she goes back to sleep. You might try singing to her."

Callisto, a smile beginning to stretch from ear to ear, silently rose from the table and went in to comfort Nera's baby.

CHAPTER TWENTY-TWO
Departure

The high priestesses firmly insisted that the girls take a short time to recover from their ordeal, so after Dido was reunited with his mistress (becoming an instant favorite of Althea and Tereus), Pandy, Alcie, and Iole were treated like little goddesses within the temple walls. Pandy told her diary everything, but when she spoke to her father, she decided to leave out a few details such as the Harpies and the pit and what exactly Jealousy looked like when she'd finally caught it. She desperately wanted to tell him about her newly discovered power over fire, but she didn't want to have to tell him how she'd found out.

Nera bought Alcie a new pair of sandals, but only gave her the left one. She spent her time breaking it in by going down the long line of supplicants with a papyrus sheet, taking pre-orders for prophecies and predictions . . . and grousing about having to get up off a soft pallet in the mornings.

"If I have a little break between visions, I'm going to ask Apollo about that mouth of yours," said Callisto.

"Yeah, yeah," Alcie said. "What about the feet? Ask him about the feet!"

Iole fed and played with the little sacrificial animals, forming a few deep attachments, only to sob bitterly as they were led to the altar.

"You know that's tradition, Iole. Part of the cycle. The gods expect it. It shows our subservience and gratitude for all that they do for us," said Nera, holding Iole as she wept, watching her favorite lamb being taken away. Iole knew the little animals were killed quickly before they were placed over the fire, not the way Callisto had almost toasted her to a crisp, but her heart still ached.

Pandy spent most of her time watching, from the shadows, the profound and sacred ceremonies taking place at the altar. Her curiosity was back in full force, but this time she knew that instead of it bringing about a dreadful result, she was gaining valuable knowledge about her culture and history. She quickly realized the high priestesses were connected to the gods, and Apollo in particular, in something more than just a spiritual way. They were the chosen ones; able to actually intercede on behalf of mankind with the immortals. The gods, Pandora thought, were all powerful. But Callisto, Ino, and Nera were holy.

She also discovered, in listening to hundreds of supplicants, that letting evil loose upon the world didn't simply mean the tiny part of the world that she knew. It meant the entire world—all of it. People had traveled from countries and lands she'd only read about: Samaria, Decapolis, China, Mauretania, and Germania Magna. Some supplicants had journeyed thousands of miles, forsaking their own temples and places of worship because they had been destroyed or looted. Pandy learned of small fights that had become wars, family members turning upon each other, atrocities done to women, children, and the elderly. A Chinese man had his rice fields burned by a rival grower . . . the man's best friend. Two sisters from Palestine had seriously hurt each other, fighting over which one actually owned a small cat. But what Pandy heard most of all, and why most of these people had come to the Temple of Apollo, the healing god, were stories of sickness. Sickness of body to be sure, but now there was such sickness of mind and soul. People were being driven mad by evil thoughts. Just when Pandy thought she couldn't feel any worse about what she'd done, she discovered she was wrong, and listening to many of the tales, she found herself adding to her vial of tears.

On the morning of their fourth day in Delphi, as the acolytes were busy preparing a farewell feast, causing much commotion around the food cupboards and drainage counter, Pandy found a quiet spot upon a long sofa among a pile of Tereus's toys. She unwrapped the map, placed fresh water into the blue bowl, and uncorked her vial of tears, watching intently as the rings rotated back and forth and finally aligned a set of strange pictures. She was immediately struck by one change. When she'd first unwrapped the map with her father, the number on the middle ring had been 180. Now it was 166.

Ino joined her briefly, as she passed through the room on her way to relieve Callisto at the altar.

"Perhaps it's the number of kilometers you've traveled? No, Athens isn't that far, is it? Perhaps it's . . . it's . . . oh, I'm sorry, Pandora, I'm just no good at guessing games."

"Thanks anyway, Ino," Pandy said.

She turned her focus to the other rings and passed the next hour poring over the brightly lit blue symbols.

Callisto was now spending her free time playing with Tereus and Althea, but after her shift that day, both Tereus and Althea were napping, so she sat down with Pandy on the sofa.

"Any luck?" she asked.

"Well, I think . . . maybe this is . . . or this thingie here might be . . . No. Nothing," Pandy said dejectedly.

"Oh," said Callisto, peering at the symbols. "Well, the only thing I can tell you is that's Egyptian."

"Huh! Really? How do you know?" Pandy cried, feeling a touch of optimism.

"I had to learn just a little of it. This temple gets so many acolyte applications from all parts of the known world; it helps to be able to read just a smattering of Phoenician, Latin, Sanskrit, and Egyptian. Ankhele?" Callisto called over her shoulder. "Would you come here for a moment?"

A young acolyte left the drainage counter, where she'd been soaking apples in lemon juice and honey. She bowed her head, not looking at Callisto.

"Yes, Priestess?" she said softly.

Pandy heard an exquisite accent in her gentle voice and looked up into eyes that were even browner than her own.

"Ankhele, can you tell us what this says?" asked Callisto, pointing to the symbols.

"Of course, Priestess." Ankhele bent down over the bowl.

"This says 'Alexandria.'"

"Do you know what this says?" asked Pandy, referring to the large symbol on the bottom ring.

"Yes, but it's strange . . . ," said Ankhele, her voice trailing off.

"What is it?" asked Pandy, holding her breath.

"It says 'Vanity.'"

"Thank you, Ankhele," said Callisto after a moment. "Please return to your preparations."

"Of course, Priestess."

"Alexandria? That's in Egypt!" Pandy said. "Well, I guess walking is out of the question. Alcie will be happy about that."

"I'm sure," Callisto replied. "You'll take the ship from Crisa, naturally."

"Oh . . . um . . . naturally. Which way is that again?"

Smiling, Callisto pointed back over her shoulder, just as Prometheus had done.

"That way . . . and sort of that way."

"Oh, right," said Pandy.

"We'll draw you a map," said Callisto with a laugh. "But not to worry; the distance is much shorter than from Athens to Delphi. Two days of walking at most. Perhaps we can get a chariot to take you partway, hmm?"

"Thank you, Callisto."

"No, Pandora . . . thank you," she said, rising and kissing Pandy lightly on her cheek. Pandora had a brief flash of her mother, almost kissing her cheek or not quite kissing the top of her head. Even knowing that Callisto had blindly wanted to kill her only a short time earlier, she had received more affection from her in the last three days than she'd felt from her mother in . . . she couldn't remember how long. She turned her face away and, hanging her head, wept silently into her robes.

That night, the altar room of the temple was closed for several hours as the high priestesses, Pandy, Iole, Alcie, and members of the Council of City Elders feasted on roast lamb, goat, and beef, mounds of rice with currants and walnuts, fresh baked flatbread smothered with olive oil and basil leaves, bowls of fruit drizzled with honey and sweet wine, cheese, hummus, boiled eggs, and apricot cakes topped with cream.

As Pandy stuffed herself, she stared up at the tall columns, remembering being hunted by Harpies only days before. Now she looked at the three high priestesses, so elegant and beautiful, so revered, and realized that she shared a bond of experience with these sacred women that couldn't be broken. How strange and wonderful, she thought; beginning to understand that everything in her world could and would change so quickly.

Iole's was the only sad face at the table as she picked up pieces of lamb and whispered, "Hector, I hope this isn't you," before chewing each bite.

As acolytes were busy passing platters and goblets, one mistakenly handed Alcie a goblet full of a rich red liquid. Alcie, her mouth full of rice, took a swallow and immediately spat out *everything*, just missing a city elder.

"Dried grapes! May Tartarus swallow you whole! Yuck!" she said. "What is this stuff?"

Callisto held up Alcie's goblet and inhaled.

"You don't want any, Alcestis?" she said, suppressing a smile.

"Harps of Hades, no! Why?"

"This is just our finest vintage of wine, that's all," she answered, as everyone broke into gales of laughter.

"Oh," Alcie said, then Alcie giggled in spite of herself.

After the feast, as they were returning to the living quarters, Pandy felt a small bit of papyrus slipped into her hand. She saw Ankhele quickly move away and begin clearing the long table.

Late that night, as Alcie, Iole, and Dido slept peacefully nearby, Pandy unfolded the note by the light of a single lamp. In uneven writing she read:

Blessed Pandora,
May Isis and Osiris guide you safely to my homeland. Please forgive my letters, Greek is still new to me. My father is the tax collector for the city of Alexandria. If you seek him out, please tell him that I have sent you. I'm certain he will help you in any way he can.

Ankhele

Refolding the note, she put it into her pouch, then reached down to the foot of her pallet and patted Dido's back. She snuggled into her pallet linens, trying to imagine what Egypt would look like, and gently drifted off.

The following morning, the girls were awakened

early so they could depart without too much notice. Though they were still full from the feast, they enjoyed a wonderful breakfast and their food pouches were filled to bursting with feast leftovers. Tereus had drawn pictures for each of them on three papyrus sheets, which they folded very carefully into their pouches. Nera wasn't quite at the end of her graveyard shift on the oracle, but she left it briefly to come say good-bye. There were tears and hugs, with promises to return to Delphi under better conditions and reciprocal vows to visit Athens on vacation. Then Pandy, Alcie, Iole, and Dido walked along the corridor toward the altar, down the flight of stairs to the side hallway, and out into the main room of the temple. As they silently slipped past the great altar, Nera, just finishing her last prediction, raised her hands high into the air as if Apollo were truly moving the spirit within her, then she winked at the girls and gave a short, deliberate flick of her wrist in farewell.

Outside, Ino, dressed in acolytes' robes and accompanied by Ankhele, led the girls past the long line already formed and across the main square. On the other side, a silver-haired man stood by a grand chariot with two stallions in the harness.

"Pandora, this is Cadmus," said Ino, "and he has agreed to take you three by chariot as far as his home, which is only a day's walk from the port city of Crisa."

Dido leapt up into the chariot and Cadmus helped

Alcie and Iole into their places as Ino bent low to embrace Pandy.

"All right, my dear," she whispered, "travel safely. Apollo is watching and his goodness spreads over you like the sun breaking through gray skies. Be well, dear one. And much success."

She squeezed Pandy's hand as the chariot started to roll down the main road toward the city entrance. Pandy shot a quick glance at Ankhele and smiled. Ankhele nodded slightly in return. The three girls looked back as long as they could at Ino, waving until she was out of sight, hidden amongst the throng of people pushing and shoving and selling and trading and waiting in the long, long line.

They traveled most of the day without stopping, enjoying the ride over the rugged countryside, especially since Alcie didn't have to walk, although eating their mid-meal of leftovers in a bouncing chariot caused most of the food to fall to the chariot bottom. The only one who really had a good meal was Dido. After midday Iole began to fret about the horses. Every few kilometers, she asked to "use the nearest bush," just to give the stallions a rest.

Apollo was dragging the sun below the horizon, turning the sky several shades of violet, when Cadmus turned the chariot down a narrow, rutted lane. Soon, they stopped at a small but beautifully kept home where a woman with a gentle face waited at the gate in the outer wall. Cadmus explained his undertaking, and his wife, Urania, made the girls welcome. Following a light supper, the three were shown to a small room with several hastily made sleeping pallets and bedded down for the night.

Several hours after midnight, however, Pandy was awakened by a peacock scream directly below their window. She bolted upright, breathing heavily, not sure at first of where she was. There was another scream, even closer. Iole sat up, looking very frightened.

"Where's Alcie?" Pandy whispered.

They both heard a thud against the wall, followed by an "Ouch!" and then Alcie stood in the doorway.

"Where have you been?" Iole asked.

"Can't a maiden get a little privacy?" Alcie said. "Figs! Okay . . . Pandy, what's with the screeching? Hera's on your side, right? Gave you the map, blah, blah, blah . . ."

"She is. She did. I don't know," said Pandy. "Are Cadmus and his wife awake?"

"I don't see any lamps on down the hallway," Iole said, now out of bed. "Pandy, what's going on?"

"Guys, don't you think if I knew I would tell . . . ," Pandy began. But she broke off suddenly as a huge peacock flew through the paneless window into their room. Pandy leapt to her feet and Dido crawled as far as he could under the pallet against the wall.

The peacock's ruby eyes glowed a sizzling red-orange and the fanned tail feathers reflected what little light there was off of shimmering diamonds, emeralds, and sapphires. Pandy hovered with Alcie and Iole in the doorway as the peacock strutted tenaciously around the room.

"Peacocks can't fly," said Alcie.

"This one can," said Pandy.

The brilliant bird found Pandy's leather carrying pouch and began pecking hard with its sharp beak, trying to shred the leather and destroy the contents inside.

Pandy remembered Nera wrapping the drying cloth around her hand in the temple. She grabbed her mother's cloak, plunging her hand deep inside the folds of fabric. She began to swing at the bird, finally delivering a blow that sent it screeching and reeling back against the wall, where it crumbled into a pile of colored dust on the floor.

"Uh-oh," said Pandora.

"What?" said Alcie and Iole together.

A blue light had appeared in the middle of the room, growing larger and brighter each instant. Alcie and Iole held fast to each other, but Pandy stood alone, trying foolishly to place herself between her friends and whatever was coming.

The blue light stretched itself sideways and downward until it reached the floor. A tasseled gold rope appeared at a diagonal and the girls could see fabric ripples forming as it transformed into a curtain complete with silver curtain rod. It hung in space for only a second, then the golden rope drew the light curtain back and they all saw the white halls and dazzling cloud formations of Mount Olympus.

Hera was walking a short distance away along a path toward the curtained opening. She held something shiny in her hand and her thin lips were pulled back in a wide smile.

"Oh, I don't want to faint again," said Alcie.

"You won't," said Iole, holding Alcie up.

The Queen of Heaven, in blue and white robes with a crown of rose gold upon her head, stepped from the pathway on Olympus through the curtain of light and into the dark little sleeping room. She smiled graciously at Pandora, but then as she turned and saw her bird in a dust pile on the floor, her face became dark and angry.

"You do this to my messenger, Pandora? This is how you repay me for my assistance?" she said, hurt and innocent.

"No, great Hera. I mean yes, but I am very sorry. I didn't know that it was a messenger. It was ripping up my—"

"Ripping? Ripping? My messenger was sent to praise you, daughter of Prometheus. Not to destroy your possessions. Did you not see the papyrus in its beak? Did you not receive my congratulations?"

"Um . . . no, mighty and wonderful Hera. I saw nothing," Pandy said, trying to think fast. She had no idea what Hera was doing, if this was some sort of game, but she wanted to be ready for anything.

"Well, if this is how you treat my small notes of acclaim," Hera said, walking over to the pile and lifting a tiny piece of rolled parchment from on top, "then I shall have to send larger signs, hmm? Like perhaps a flood from the Gulf of Corinth upon which ships will ride, their sails bearing the words, 'Well done, Pandora!' Would you like that? Will that be necessary from now on?"

Hera held out the note from the pile of dust; a note Pandy knew had not been there before. Before Pandy could take it, however, it vanished in midair.

"I'll just deliver the message personally," Hera said, as if it were the best thing anyone had ever said in the history of the world. "Most high praise, Pandora! You bring honor to the House of Prometheus!"

Hera's words were wonderful, but just as she had on Olympus, Pandy again had the sense of something terrible underneath and an image flashed before Pandy's eyes: black snakes swimming under sweet cream.

"Thank you, wise Hera," said Pandy.

"Oh, I'm not the wise one, dearest. That's Athena. But then, you don't really know her all that well, do you? Now, I've also brought you this . . ." She held out her other hand, which was full of shiny gold coins.

Pandy had never seen coins like them; their edges were not like Grecian coins and the symbols imprinted were of a bird and a large eye. All at once, Pandy knew where she'd seen these symbols before: they were very similar to the ones she'd read on the map, but Hera had clasped her hands together and was smiling broadly again.

"It's a clue!" she whispered conspiratorially, absolutely delighted with herself. "Zeus would be furious if he knew I was here, helping you more than I already have, which is considerable. But I felt that such tremendous effort and success deserved a teensy reward. After all, daughter of Prometheus, not all plagues will be so easy to capture. So that's a clue to your next location."

"We already know what our next—," Alcie blurted from the shadows.

"Thank you, most generous queen!" said Pandy, not even looking behind her, but hoping she was quick and loud enough to cover Alcie's blunder.

"I'm sure you'll be able decipher my clue . . . you're such a clever little maiden," said Hera, ignoring Alcie and looking deep into Pandy's eyes. Where before Pandy had sensed dislike from Hera, she now felt she was the recipient of a deep loathing.

"Thank you. Thank you for everything."

"Good-bye, Pandora Atheneus Andromaeche Helena. I'm sure I'll see you before long."

Smiling sweetly, Hera waved her hand and the dust

pile flew up and through the curtain of light with a loud screech. Hera turned on her large heels and walked back on the golden path of Olympus. An instant later, the curtain of light disappeared.

After that, no one was sleepy in the least, so Pandy, Alcie, and Iole spent the rest of the night plotting their strategy upon arriving in Crisa. Iole and Alcie would find an inn with a comfortable room and Pandy, with Dido as protection, would book their passage on a ship to Egypt.

"With what?" bemoaned Alcie. "We don't have that kind of money!"

"Yes, we do," said Pandy. And she held up the Egyptian coins.

"Gold is gold."

"Gods! Do you think Hera realized how much she gave you?" said Iole.

"I don't know," Pandy replied. "She's pretty sharp."

They talked for hours, about their adventure so far and Iole's remarkable healing.

"That's twice now, you know," Iole said. "Once on Crete and once in his very own temple. Someday, I'd like to thank Apollo!"

"Hey, guys," Pandy said, pulling out the map and pointing to the single number on the middle ring, "take a look at this. Wasn't this a different number when we were on the road? 160 . . . something?"

"Why, what's the biggie?" Alcie said.

"Well," Pandy said, glancing at the number, "now it's 164—whoa! It was 166 two days ago!"

Pandy stared at Alcie, who stared right back. Then they both looked at Iole, her eyes locked on the map, her mind working furiously.

"It's simple," she said at length. "It's a counter. And if my calculations are correct, it's counting the number of days we have left."

"Almost twenty days have gone by," Pandy said, "and there's only one evil in the box."

"You could look at it like that, I suppose," said Iole, sensing her friend's distress. "But I prefer to ruminate that we have over five whole moons to do this!"

Pandy smiled, but the three remained silent . . . and no one slept.

At daybreak, Urania poked her head into their tiny room and found each girl already dressed and packed to leave. She scurried to the food cupboards and prepared a first-meal of boiled eggs, vegetables, and grain cakes with hibiscus honey. Cadmus told them that Crisa was two large hills away and if they hurried, they'd reach it shortly after midday.

The girls thanked their hosts and left feeling refreshed, even with such little sleep.

"Why didn't they wake up last night?" asked Alcie, back on the main chariot road.

"Why do you think?" said Iole sincerely. "The gods can appear to whomever they want. Hera is magnificent, Pandy. And boy, does she like you!"

"Yes," said Pandy, thinking about Jealousy steaming away inside the little wooden box and Hera's last words, something about all of the plagues not being so easy to capture. "Yes, I am blessed."

The four walked on, cresting one hill and then another, until at last the city of Crisa lay below them. Pandy looked beyond the city walls to the Gulf of Corinth, spreading out before her like a beautiful deep blue blanket. She smiled, looking at the tall ships in the harbor, one of which, she knew, would take them all to Egypt.

EPILOGUE

In her fine apartments, the Queen of Heaven sat at her looking glass, brushing her red hair with long, fast, harsh stokes; curious and livid at the same time.

"She's getting help! I can feel it," Hera said, cleaning her brush of the massive amounts of hair she'd ripped from her head (all of which, of course, instantly grew back).

"I suppose it doesn't really matter. There's no chance of her success. Not with the things I have in store for her. But still . . . the other girl . . . the child who walks oddly. She babbled that they already knew where to look for the second plague. That map is unreadable to a silly little maiden, I don't care how many friends she has traveling with her!"

"What are you going to do?" came a soft voice from a divan in the shadows.

"Well, I'm having too much fun watching the little

fool struggle to really care, so I suppose I'll see where she goes and just continue to poke at her a bit. After all, she's only been at this a little less than one moon. I've got over five moons left to mislead her all over the planet. It is not yet time for you or me to put her in mortal danger. High priestesses and Harpies have been doing that just fine for the past few days . . . and there's more to come of that kind of sport, you can be sure. Do you know what they do to trespassers and infidels in Egypt?"

Hera, who'd witnessed such destruction and mayhem since the world began and had caused much of it, shuddered in spite of herself.

"All right. All done. How do I look?"

There was a laugh from the shadows.

"How else could the wife of Zeus look? You will outshine all others."

"I'm so glad Zeus finally decided to make the others throw me a surprise party. How's this . . . will I look surprised?"

Hera unhinged her jaw and widened her eyes. She looked more terrified and grotesque than genuinely surprised.

"Perfect. Shall we go? They're probably all in place by now."

"Yes, let's," Hera said. She lumbered toward the door

of her apartments, stopping only briefly as the figure rose off the divan to join her.

"What do you know about any other help that she's getting?" she asked.

"I've told you everything already."

"Yes, yes . . . Athena and Hephaestus and the silly net. I expected something like that from those goody-goodies. But you'll continue to tell me everything that you hear or see, won't you?"

"Darling, after the wealth and power you've promised me . . . the two of us ruling heaven and earth side by side . . . you know I will! Trust me."

They moved out of Hera's rooms, Hera in front, her blue and white robes flowing behind her. The figure who'd been in the shadows now stepped into the brilliantly lit hallway, leaving only a smattering of autumn leaves and icicles melting on the floor to show that she'd been there at all.

GLOSSARY

Acropolis (uh-CROP-o-lis): the tallest point of land in Athens upon which stood the Parthenon.

Aeolus (AY-o-lus): King of the Winds; a god who lived on earth on a floating island called Aeolia.

Aphrodite (af-ro-DI-tee): Goddess of Love and Beauty.

Apollo (uh-POL-oh): God of Music, Poetry, Light, Truth, and the Healing Arts. Often called the "Sun-God," it is Apollo, in his magnificent chariot, who pulls the sun across the heavens each day.

Ares (AIR-ees): God of War; he is the son of Zeus and Hera, both of whom, legend says, absolutely hated him.

Artemis (AR-teh-miss): twin sister of Apollo; often called the "Lady of Wild Things," she was huntsman-in-chief of the gods. She was also the protector of youth and young things everywhere; and, commonly, the primary goddess of the moon.

Athena (uh-THEE-nuh): Goddess of Wisdom and Reason. She has no mother, but instead sprang from Zeus's head—fully grown and in full battle dress. She is a fierce warrior-goddess, wily and cunning. She is Zeus's favorite child.

Atlas (AT-lass): one of the original Titans and, in some myths, Prometheus's brother. Zeus condemned Atlas to bear the crushing vault of the heavens on his shoulders forever. (Often he is portrayed as also having to hold up the earth as well, but that's just illogical. I mean, think about it, where would he stand? Hmm?)

Bacchanalia (BOK-an-all-ee-a): a loud, noisy party.

Bellerophon (bell-AIR-o-fon): hero who tamed the winged horse, Pegasus, and slew the dreaded Chimera.

Caduceus (ca-DOO-see-us): a staff carried by Hermes with two snakes intertwined around it, meeting at the top beneath a pair of wings; the inspiration for the symbol used by doctors or hospitals today.

Calydonian Boar (cal-ih-DON-ih-an): an enormous boar that terrorized the Calydon countryside.

centaurs (SEN-tors): creatures with the upper body of a man and the lower body of a horse.

Cerberus (SIR-burr-us): an enormous dog with three heads (some accounts also say a dragon's tail) who guards the gates of Hades.

Chimera (key-MER-uh): a mythical monster with the body of a goat, the tail of a snake, and the head of a lion. Oh, and it also breathed fire.

Crete (KREET): the largest Greek island.

Cronus (CROW-nus): a Titan and the father of Zeus, Hestia, Hera, Hades, Poseidon, and Demeter. He swallowed his children whole as soon as they were born, believing the prophecy that one of his children would overthrow him. When Zeus was born, however, Rhea, his mother, wrapped a stone in a blanket and gave it to

Cronus, hiding the baby Zeus on Crete. When Zeus was grown, he forced his father to disgorge all of his brothers and sisters. Then ensued the battle between the Titans and the Olympians for control of the heavens and earth.

Cyclops (SIGH-clops): defines either the race or one of the race of ancient giants who had only one eye located in the middle of their forehead.

Delphi (DELL-figh): a city in Greece, site of the famous Oracle of Apollo (also called the Oracle at Delphi and the Temple of Apollo).

Demeter (de-MEE-ter): sister of Zeus, Goddess of Agriculture and the Harvest; patron of agriculture, planting, crops, health, birth, and marriage.

Dionysus (dye-oh-NIGH-sus): above all else, God of Wine and Theater, and, with Demeter, also a God of Agriculture.

dryads (DRY-ads): nymphs that lived in trees; when the trees died, so did the dryads.

Eros (EE-ros): son of Aphrodite, and the God of Love. Eros is more commonly known as his Roman counterpart, Cupid.

Euphrates (eew-FRAY-tees): a large river in southwestern Asia.

Gorgons (GOR-gons): three sisters (two were immortal) usually described as dragonlike creatures with wings, brass hands (in some accounts), and live snakes for hair. Looking directly upon any of the Gorgons would instantly turn the viewer to stone.

Hades (HAY-dees): Zeus's brother and ruler of the underworld (the land of the dead, also called Hades).

Harpies (HAR-pees): "the hounds of Zeus"; winged dragons with serpents' tails, razor-sharp claws, and hooked beaks. In addition to their fearful appearance, the Harpies left the foulest stench imaginable in their wake.

Hephaestus (heh-FEST-us): God of Fire and the Forge. He is the armorer and smith of the gods. He is the only god to be born ugly and misshapen, yet his wife is Aphrodite.

Hera (HAIR-uh): Zeus's wife and sister. She is the Queen of Heaven and is the protector of marriage, married women, and childbearing. Two words describe Hera: jealous and petty. Of course, that might be because Zeus's many affairs have plagued her since the creation of mythology.

Hercules (HER-cue-lees): a demigod (his father was Zeus) and the greatest and most famous of the ancient Greek heroes. Hercules had to perform twelve almost impossible labors as penance for killing his wife in a (Hera-induced) fit of madness.

Hermes (HER-mees): the messenger of the gods, the swiftest in action and thought. He was known as "the Master Thief" (having stolen Apollo's herd of cows on the day he was born) and was God of Commerce and the Market, the protector of traders.

hydra (HIGH-dra): a huge water snake with nine separate heads, one of which was immortal. To kill the Lernaean hydra was one of the twelve labors of Hercules.

Medea (meh-DEE-uh): a Greek princess who killed her two children when her husband fell in love with another woman.

Medusa (meh-DOO-suh): a hideous, snake-haired Gorgon; she was banished to a rocky island where she lived with her two immortal Gorgon "sisters." She was killed by Perseus, who cut off her head and gave it to Athena, who then placed it in the center of her shield, also called her *aegis*.

Morpheus (MORE-fee-us): God of Dreams; Morpheus would often appear in dreams as your loved ones.

Nemean Lion (NEE-me-an): an enormous lion, killed by Hercules with his bare hands as the first of his twelve labors.

Olympus (o-LIM-puss): an enormous mountain in northeast Greece, close to the coast of the Aegean Sea; at its summit is the home of the twelve Olympian gods.

oracle (OR-a-kull): there are three distinctive definitions: a person who sees and predicts the future; a prophecy or prediction as told by a temple priest, priestess, or seer; a shrine or temple where a god was consulted.

Pan (PAN): Hermes' son; God of Goatherds and Shepherds. Pan is part animal, with goat horns and a goat's hindquarters, legs, and hoofs. He is an excellent musician, having created the panpipes.

Parnassus (par-NASS-us), also *Parnassos:* a mountain in central Greece.

Parthenon (PAR-thuh-non): standing atop the Acropolis, the Parthenon was the primary temple to the city's patron goddess, Athena.

Pegasus (PEG-a-suss): a beautiful, white winged horse, born from the blood flowing from Medusa's neck after Perseus beheaded her.

Persephone (per-SEH-pho-nee): daughter of Demeter, unwilling wife of Hades. Persephone spends six months of the year in the underworld with her husband, during which Demeter turns her back on the world, which is why we have autumn and winter. When Persephone is with Demeter, she rejoices, giving us spring and summer.

Perseus (PER-see-us): a young hero who killed the Gorgon Medusa, by looking at her reflection in Athena's metal shield to avoid her eyes, which could turn him to stone.

phileo (fill-EH-oh): deep love from a friend to a friend, or from a father to a daughter.

Poseidon (pos-EYE-don): brother to Zeus and Lord of the Sea.

Prometheus (pro-MEE-thee-us): a Titan who fought on the side of the gods in the battle for supremacy over the earth and heavens. He also stole fire from Zeus when Zeus refused to share it with mankind. For this he was chained to a rock where a giant eagle would feast on his liver during the day, only to have it grow back at night.

satyr (SAY-ter): a woodland deity, very often described as a cross between a man and a goat. Often connected with Dionysus, satyrs like women . . . a lot.

Sirens (SIGH-rens): creatures with beautiful, enchanting voices; they would lure sailors on passing ships to their deaths with their captivating songs. They inhabited a small island in the middle of the sea, but no description of them is known, because no one who looked upon them ever returned.

Stymphalian Birds (stim-FAY-lee-an): many accounts say these were flesh-eating birds. Hercules shot them as his sixth labor.

Tartarus (TAR-tar-uss): a terrible place in the underworld—even lower than Hades. It is described as being so hidden from sunlight and so deep in the earth that it is surrounded by three separate layers of night, which in turn surround a bronze wall, which then encompasses Tartarus. Sometimes it is described as a dank and wretched pit engulfed in murky gloom. In other descriptions, it is a place of white-hot flame.

Titan (TIE-tan): a race of giant gods who ruled supreme over heaven and earth until they were overthrown in a fierce battle with Zeus and the other Olympians. The Titans that sided with Zeus in battle, he rewarded; those that did not, he imprisoned in Tartarus.

Tiresias (tye-REE-see-us): fictional, but named for a famous blind Greek prophet.

Zeus (ZOOS): the supreme ruler, chief among all the gods, wielder of the mighty lightning bolt (sometimes called thunderbolt). His power is greater than that of all the other gods combined. He is often portrayed as falling in love with one woman after another, which infuriates his wife, Hera.

ACKNOWLEDGMENTS

Thanks to Elizabeth Hailey, Kim O'Bannon, Elizabeth Harris, Melissa McNeeley, Jamie Wooten, Nicholas Hope, Barbara Olsen, Craig Newhouse, Peter Renaday, Madeleine Pellegren, Dan Schneider, Wenzel Jones, Christina Carlisi, Phyllis Kramer, Brooks Adams, Meg Brogan, Mary McGuire, Trista Delamere, William Sterchi, Rene, Charlotte, Sybil and Martha Pallace, Kelli Coleman, Betty Buckner, Gerald Brennan, Claudette Sutherland, Warren Cowan, Karen Smith, Richard Overton, Katy Dowdalls, Frank Crim, Mary Mazzocco, Boots Hart, Edith Eig, Ezra Buzzington, Peter Gref, Marc Rosenbush, Todd McClaren, Michael John Derricott, Michael and Becca Hennesy, Brian Hennesy, Jennifer Griffin, Camden Toy, Mary Lou Belli, Sarina Rantfl, Pavlin Lange, Dace Lavelle, Tony Pines, Emily Webster, and Susan Blu for their time, comments, laughter, and, in some cases, sheer astonishment.

Special thanks to Leah Miller for her top-ten list; Minnie Schedeen, who knows more than most; Dino Carloftas at Metro and Nancy Gallt, the two best agents a gal could have; Elizabeth Schonhorst, editor extraordinaire, who laughs at what I say and gently clarifies what I write; my mother, Ramona, and my aunt Barbara, who read everything with love and clear eyes; Sarabeth for her faith, love, wisdom, and for always reminding me of the source and supply; Scott Hennesy for laughing (which means a lot); Harriet for her encouragement; Kel, who rushed right over; Josie, my "sister," for pronouncing it "poddy"; and Rosie, of course . . . always.

And, finally, thank you to Michael Scott for saying, "You know what this *really* is . . . ?"

READ ON FOR A SNEAK PEEK AT
PANDORA'S NEXT MYTHIC MISADVENTURE

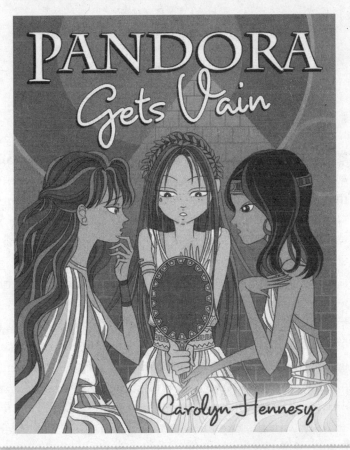

PANDORA
Gets Vain

Carolyn Hennesy

CHAPTER ONE

Storm

7:56 p.m.

A storm such as Pandy had never seen hit three days after they reached the open sea. The waves were as tall as temple pillars and the winds were shredding holes in the enormous black-and-white striped mainsail. Hard rain was pouring from the sky with the ferocity of a waterfall, and the ship had been careening, skidding, and lurching violently ever since it had passed the jagged outcropping of rock that formed the coastline of western Greece, just past the city of Methone.

Almost an hour earlier, as the first gusts of wind began to swirl about the ship, the captain insisted that his passengers go below deck immediately. Pandy and her friends, Alcie and Iole, had come up topside for a breath of fresh air only moments before. They tried to comply with the captain's orders, but as they took their first steps from the bow toward the small set of stairs at the stern, the winds immediately shifted, slapping them back against the railings and almost blowing them into the water. For the last forty-five minutes, the hurricane had pinned all three girls and several well-seasoned sailors to the railings, the huge mast, and the cargo crates that were tied down to the deck. The black clouds made it difficult for Pandy to keep her friends in sight. She knew Alcie would be able to hold on; in fact, Alcie's recent affliction of having two left feet had somehow made her able to negotiate her way around the ship. Instead of constantly veering off to her right as she did on land, the gentle glide of the hull over the water had miraculously straightened out Alcie's stride and before the storm had descended, Alcie was seriously considering becoming a sailor. Now, Pandy could just make out Alcie against the mast, her hands intertwined in the sail ropes, riding out the storm like it was merely a light breeze.

Iole was a much different story, and it was only when the first bolts of lightning began striking the water all around them that Pandy saw her little friend was in serious trouble. Iole had been thrown against the railings easily with the first gust. Now her thin arms and legs were slipping through the large gaps between the railing posts. The rain, the constant spray of seawater, and the dip of the ship as it crested wave after wave was making it impossible for Iole to hang on. She couldn't keep a grip on the railing posts; they were too thick and the wood was gummy and slimy from years of exposure to the salty sea air.

Pandy's place on the deck was precarious enough; she was being tossed about between two large packing crates, and she could feel her shoulders and legs beginning to bruise. But she'd wrapped her arms around the ropes that held the crates to the deck and she felt that, though she was going to be black and blue, she was fairly safe. Now, however, with lightning illuminating Iole almost half overboard, Pandy knew that if she didn't get to Iole fast, she'd be less one best friend.

Pandy freed her arms from the ropes and crept forward on her hands and knees over the slippery deck toward Alcie and the mast. Alcie's body was turned in such a way that she didn't yet see Iole was in trouble. Pandy screamed at the top of her lungs, pointing toward the railing. Alcie squirmed around the mast to look and shrieked, sticking one of her left feet out for Pandy to grab hold of. Pandy pulled herself over Alcie's leg, inching her way up to a standing position, and began trying to untie the heavy rope coiled around the mast.

"What are you doing?" yelled Alcie.

"I'm gonna try to get this to Iole!" Pandy yelled back.

Suddenly a rough hand yanked the end of the rope out of her grasp and grabbed her forearm.

"That rope holds the mainsail! You could bring down the whole ship, you fool!" said one of two sailors who'd also been pinned against the mast by the winds.

"My friend is going to be killed!" Pandy screamed, pointing to the railing.

"Too bad for her," yelled the other sailor, lightning flashing on his grimy, toothless face. "But you're not going to wreck the *Peacock!*"

"What?" gasped Pandy, taking in a mouthful of salt water. "What did you say?"

"The *Peacock* has weathered worse than this and you stupid maidens are not going to do anything to destroy her," snarled the first sailor, his hand still clapped around Pandy's.

"Great Gods," Pandy thought, "that's it!" The name of the ship was the *Peacock* and that could mean only one thing. *One thing!*

Hera, the Queen of Heaven, whose primary symbol was the peacock, had sent this storm. Pandy was never more sure of anything in her life. Hera had somehow seen to it that Pandy and her friends had boarded this ship, and now she was bent on sending it to the bottom of the sea. Why oh why had she not recognized the danger before they got onboard? Had she even noticed the name of the ship?

At that moment, the *Peacock* fell into a deep trough in the waves and the sailor released his grasp on

Pandy's arm to brace himself against the mast. Pandy went tumbling—flying was more like it—toward Iole and the railing. She hit the railing so hard that she thought she'd cracked a rib. She was about to be tossed to the other side of the ship when she saw Iole's hand just inches away. Instantly she grabbed on to it, and the force of the lurch and Pandy's extra weight helped drag Iole back on board a bit. But there was nothing else to hold on to, nothing to tie them down. The packing crates were too far away. Alcie had attempted Pandy's idea of using the mast rope, but she was now pinned by the two sailors, who kept her restrained even though she was trying to bite them.

Iole looked at Pandy, unable to speak, her eyes red from crying and salt water.

"I need a rope," Pandy thought, now completely desperate. "All I need is a stupid *rope*!"

The following instant, a flash of lightning carved the face of the great goddess Athena in the air precisely in front of Pandy's nose. Athena looked directly at Pandy and winked at her.

And then Pandy had an idea.

Only a week before, Athena had given Pandy a magic rope, one that would grow longer or shorter, thicker or thinner, depending on what was needed. All Pandy had to do was ask the rope to do something and the next moment it was done. But each time she'd used it before, the rope had actually been in her hands. Now the rope was coiled securely inside her leather carrying pouch, which was stowed in her cabin safely below deck.

There was no way she could physically get to it, not without letting go of Iole, and Pandy knew she'd never make it below deck and back in time.

But Athena had not appeared to her just to give her a wink.

"Rope . . . come to me . . . ," Pandy began to mutter under her breath.

"Rope . . . come to me . . . *now!*" She said the words again and again, without the faintest notion if her summoning was working.

As the *Peacock* rode up another crest, Pandy and Iole were almost vertical to the deck. Only Iole's foot, hooked around one of the railing posts, and Pandy's left arm, hooked around another post, kept them from falling down toward the stern of the ship.

"Rope . . . come to me . . . I need you . . . now!" Pandy said again and again.

The ship plunged down into the trough and Pandy lost her grip on Iole's wrist as Iole, screaming, slipped halfway through the railing.

As Pandy was thrown upside down with the force of the plummet, a bolt of lightning struck close to the passageway opening. Pandy's head jerked toward the flash and her eye caught sight of something thin and silvery on deck. The magic rope was snaking its way toward her from the passageway opening. The sailors trapped on deck didn't even notice; they were too busy trying to save their own lives.

"Faster!" she cried. Instantly the rope was in her hands.

"Longer . . . thicker!" she yelled and the rope obeyed.

Iole screamed again. At least Pandy thought it was Iole. It might have been the giant peacock that had appeared suddenly, hovering in the air for an instant over her head, a brilliant sapphire blue and ruby red bird, screeching at the top of its voice.

Iole was almost gone, only her feet, hooked to two of the railing posts, were still visible.

"Catch Iole now!" Pandy yelled. One end of the rope flew from Pandy's hands and disappeared overboard.

"Bring her back!" Pandy cried, not knowing if the rope could even understand more complex commands. But the next moment Iole was on deck, the rope wound about her waist and shoulders in a beautiful little harness.

"Hold us both to the railing!" Pandy said, and the rope stretched itself to be able to firmly secure both Pandy and Iole to the posts, and wrapped itself around the two girls with a series of intricate knots.

In that instant, Pandy realized that if the ship held together they would all be safe.

Then the storm stopped. Completely.

Within minutes, the sky was clear and blue. The coastline of Greece was visible once again and the jagged rock formations were in exactly the same spot as before the storm. Which, Pandy knew, meant that the *Peacock* hadn't moved at all. The Ionian Sea lay before them smooth as a looking glass.

"Rope . . . let us go," Pandy said softly. The rope released her and Iole instantly. "Smaller . . . very small," she said, and the rope nestled itself into the palm of her hand. She tucked it behind her silver girdle.

The sailors began to crawl from their hiding places all over the deck. The two who had restrained Alcie immediately backed away, because she was still nipping at them.

"Come on, Iole," Pandy said, helping her waterlogged friend to her feet. They stumbled over to Alcie, standing against the mast, her hands still intertwined with the ropes. Alcie was swearing at the sailors who'd held her captive, demonstrating her other affliction: anytime she cursed (which was a lot), it came out as . . . fruit.

"Figs! Lemons! Pears to you both!" she called to the now-laughing sailors, her arms over her head.

"Alcie . . . you can let go now, you know," Pandy said.

"Oh!" Alcie said with a start. "Oh, right!"

The three girls dragged themselves past the crew members now checking the ship, the deck, and the cargo for damage. The men were calling out that the storm was bad all right but they'd seen worse, each one trying to outdo the others with tall tales, as the girls slipped down into the passageway below deck.

Safe and warm once again, the girls locked their cabin door and took off their soaked outer togas, hanging them on the ends of their sleeping cots to dry. No one spoke for a long time.

"What was that?" Iole said finally.

"Duh!" said Alcie, sitting on her cot with her back against the hull of the ship. "Only the worst storm *I've* ever seen."

"It was more than that," said Iole, turning to Pandy, "wasn't it?"

"I don't know. I-I think . . . ," Pandy stammered. "Yes. It was more than just a bad storm."

"What? What do you mean more?" Alcie asked.

"Pandy . . . I saw the peacock in the air," Iole said.

"What peacock?" said Alcie.

"If the peacock had tried to help in some way, or calm the winds," Iole went on, "but it was screeching . . ."

"I know . . . it's a sign of some sort," Pandy replied.

"Sign? What sign?" Alcie barked.

"Alcie, just listen, okay?" said Pandy, curling her legs up underneath her and rubbing her side where she'd smashed into the railing. Dido, her dog, had been severely tossed about in their cabin during the storm and now he laid his head, a small cut just above his right eye, in Pandy's lap. "If I knew exactly what was going on, believe me, I'd tell you. I know you guys didn't have to come with me on this quest, and you know I'd never keep anything from you."

She dropped her voice to a whisper.

"Hera sent the storm. I'd bet all our food supplies on it. Did you see how quickly the storm cleared up once there was no chance that Iole or I would be killed?"

"But why, Pandy?" said Iole. "She's the one who gave you the map when you were up on Olympus in front of Zeus. She's the one who took pity on you and convinced Zeus not to boil you in oil, but to let you come on this search. She gave you the gold coins as a clue to go to Egypt."

"Look," Pandy sighed, "all I know is that Hera says one thing and means another. And she doesn't like me; she pretends to, but she doesn't. At all."

She put the small coil of rope back in her leather carrying pouch.

"Why wouldn't she like you?" asked Alcie.

"I don't know yet," Pandy shot back, then she dropped her voice again. "The only thing I'm pretty sure of is that whatever she's doing . . . it's going to get worse."

DONALD AGNELLI

Carolyn Hennesy

is also the author of *Pandora Gets Vain* and *Pandora Gets Lazy*. A Los Angeles native, she has more than twenty-five years' experience in the entertainment industry, having appeared in more than two hundred films, TV shows, commercials, and live stage productions. In addition to her full-time acting and writing careers, Ms. Hennesy also teaches improvisational comedy and has become a flying trapeze artist. She lives in the Los Angeles area.

www.carolynhennesy.com

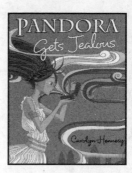 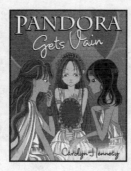 

FIVE DELINQUENT GIRL SCOUTS,
ONE SECRET CITY BENEATH MANHATTAN,
AND A BUTT-KICKING SUPERSPY . . .

Welcome to the world of **KIKI STRIKE!**

"If Harry Potter lived in New York City, he'd have a mad crush on 14-year-old Kiki Strike." —*Vanity Fair*

www.kikistrike.com

BLOOMSBURY
www.bloomsburyusa.com